A DISTURBING PROSPECT

RIVER REAPERS MOTORCYCLE CLUB, BOOK 1

ELIZABETH BARONE

ALSO BY ELIZABETH BARONE

Any Other Love

Crazy Comes in Threes

Just One More Minute

The Nanny with the Skull Tattoos

Sade on the Wall

The Stairs Between Us

RIVER REAPERS SERIES

A Disturbing Prospect

A Risky Prospect

SOUTH OF FOREVER SERIES

Twisted Broken Strings

Diving Into Him

Savannah's Song

What Happens on Tour

Visit **elizabethbaronebooks.com** to purchase!

MAIETTA INK

A Disturbing Prospect

River Reapers MC, Book 1

Copyright © 2019 by Elizabeth Campbell, writing as Elizabeth Barone

All Rights Reserved

1st Edition

Cover photography by cokacoka/Deposit Photos and Dunraven Productions/Period Images

Cover designed by Natasha Snow

ISBN 978-0-9912838-7-3

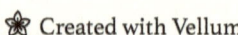 Created with Vellum

A DISTURBING PROSPECT

Until now, Olivia has survived by sticking to two simple rules: love 'em then leave 'em, and live out loud. But her odds—which were pretty good—change when Cliff walks out of prison and into her life. With his long dark hair, gentle eyes, and secrets, she's dying to unlock him.

Cliff is a survivor, too, and he needs Olivia's help learning how to live again. But his past catches up with him when he joins the local biker club, the River Reapers. A lifetime membership comes with its own baggage.

Olivia should stay far, far away from him. She shouldn't get skin to skin with him in the back of someone else's car, but she does. She definitely shouldn't get to know the man behind the mugshot, but for the first time in a long parade of one-night stands, she wants to. And she shouldn't fall for him, but she does. Except their entwined pasts may doom their love before it even begins.

For everyone who's ever taken your power back.

FOREWORD

A Disturbing Prospect is the darkest book I've written so far. There were some wrongs that I really needed to right—injustices that should've been paid for but weren't. What you hold in your hands is the result of emotions I've carried inside me for a long time.

Some of the themes in this book might make some people uncomfortable, and may even be triggering for people with personal trauma. I've made a list of potential trigger warnings that I'm including here.

For the sake of realism, I've depicted biker culture from my own experience and understanding. Although that culture and its attitudes toward women is changing, it has a long way to go. My goal for this book and its subsequent series is to help change that mentality.

TRIGGER WARNINGS

Not only is there a body count, but the book also deals with some real-life nightmares that I've longed to fight back against. Some of these themes may trigger personal trauma.

I needed to tell the story in my heart and right some wrongs, but I'd also never want anyone to suffer because of my words. None of these themes are gratuitously presented in the book, and my vigilante bikers always prevail. Still, I want my readers to be safe, so here is a list of potential triggers.

Animals: There's no pet death in *A Disturbing Prospect*, but an animal is harmed.

Biker Culture: Let's be real—biker culture is misogynistic as fuck. I wanted to portray that realistically, while also incorporating some changes. There's some biker slang and characters who treat women as property in this book.

Childhood Sexual Abuse: Some of the characters have a history of being sexually abused as children. None of their memories are described, but there is mention of it having happened.

Drugs: There is brief mention of selling and use of drugs.

Self-Injury: A character catches a glimpse of another character's self-mutilated arms.

Sexual Assault: One of the recurring themes in this series is violence against women and children. (One of the other recurring themes, however, is justice for that violence.) There are some hints of past sexual assault throughout *A Disturbing Prospect*.

Stalking: A character mercilessly stalks and taunts another character throughout *A Disturbing Prospect*.

Violence: All of the good guys in this series are vigilantes—antiheroes who take justice into their own hands. There is blood, fighting, gun violence, and a villain body count.

If you feel that you won't be safe reading *A Disturbing Prospect*, please don't risk your health. As a sexual assault survivor and someone with PTSD, I wish every book came with a list of trigger warnings. No book is worth risking your safety.

Please also note that I don't necessarily condone or endorse the themes contained in this book.

If you've read *A Disturbing Prospect* and feel that I may have missed something, please email me at elizabethbaronebooks@gmail.com.

1

CLIFF

The second the sun touches my skin on the other side of the barbed wire chain link fence, I am truly free. It doesn't matter that I have to meet with my probation officer, or that I don't exactly have any place to go. All that's important is I'm not rotting within those cement walls anymore.

My twenty years are finally up.

The taxi idles, puffs of exhaust eddying into the cold February air. The dead of winter is a shitty time to be homeless, but even that thought doesn't dampen my spirits. Prison wasn't terrible, but it wasn't like being outside. Inside, I was just a caged animal throwing myself at the bars, bruising and bloodying myself in defiance. I was in segregation more times than I can count, and I'm lucky I got out five years early.

I'd kiss the fucking ground if the guy behind the wheel wasn't already eyeing me warily.

I slide into the backseat, warmth from the heater enveloping me. A sigh nearly escapes my lips. It's been so long since I was really, truly warm.

Through the rearview mirror, the taxi driver continues to question my sanity. He isn't prejudiced. "Where to, sir?" he asks, his voice void of any accent. He could be from Anywhere, America. Actually, the United States could've sunk into the bowels of hell while I was inside, for all I know. Maybe this accent is the new norm.

I squint at him, trying to decide whether I've lost my fucking mind or if this is really the way things are now. He even looks racially ambiguous, with a broad hooked nose, green eyes, and olive skin.

The newspapers I managed to get my hands on were always old, and the old men hogged the lone fucking TV all day. I have no clue what's going on in the world. Or where I'm going.

Maybe he takes pity on me, because his eyes soften and he clears his throat. "How long have you been in, sir?"

I really wish he'd stop with the *sir*, but it's better than what I've been called. What I *am*. Who. "Twenty years," I tell him.

He nods real slow, then he rubs his chin, the stubble not quite poking through yet. It's too early in the day. It's another difference between us. My goatee is scratchy. I didn't have time to shave this morning.

"Well," he says finally. "We have a woman president."

This I knew. I start to tell him that I haven't been living in a fucking hole, but that would not be true. "Isn't that something," I reply.

He shoves the taxi into drive and pulls away from the only home I've ever known. I've been inside longer than I'd been alive when I went in.

A sliver of panic creeps in. I don't know how to cook or how to drive a car. It seems ridiculous, pathetic. And I still don't know where I'm going. I have no one on the outside. At least, I don't think so.

During the first year, I had visitors. Then they trickled into phone calls, faded into letters, until finally, nothing. I don't blame them. Twenty years is a long time, and Pennsylvania isn't exactly close to home.

The taxi driver takes me to a Days Inn. I don't even bother looking through the glass as we drive through the small town. There's not a damn thing here.

I use most of the only cash I have left to buy a room for the night, and when I leave the lobby to find my room, the taxi is already gone. Blinking into the winter gloom, it starts to sink in that I don't have any friends, inside or out.

I'm a goddamn statistic.

But the room has a shower that doesn't run cold after two minutes, and I take a half hour to revel in my first real taste of freedom. The hot water sluices over hard muscle I've been careful to build and maintain. My own mother probably wouldn't recognize me.

After I step out, I clear the mirror with a hand and take a good look. It's been a while since I looked at my reflection in something other than a mirror that more closely resembled a dented paper towel dispenser. In the pen, everything is constructed with safety in mind, carefully evaluated to ensure that even the simplest of tools can't be converted into deadly weapons.

But anything can be a weapon.

Anything.

Even my bare hands.

The goatee doesn't surprise me. It's familiar and has kept my face warm for two decades. It's the crow's feet at the corners of my brown eyes that make me pause. I'm only thirty-eight, but even though I don't feel it, I look it. Maybe even five years older.

A frown creases my forehead.

It really shouldn't matter. I'm not entering any beauty pageants anytime soon. And any woman who might be interested would be quick to run in the opposite direction the second she heard about my record.

She'd be careless not to.

I drape the towel over the hook on the back of the door and stalk out bare as the day I was born. There's no one here to see me, and I'm not too keen on the idea of changing back into those clothes. They were donated to the prison. Never were mine. The clothes I wore the day I was cuffed are long gone, tucked into some forgotten evidence bin or maybe even burned, since the case was pretty quickly closed.

There was no point in pleading innocence.

I sit on the bed and eye the phone. I might have one friend out there. It's a long shot, really. But maybe not that long.

Snatching the phone from its cradle, I pause. Try to remember how to call someone whose number you don't have. I have no fucking idea. I slam the receiver down, wishing I had a pack of cigarettes. Or even one cigarette would do.

I'm about to throw back on those moldy old clothes when I remember. I can call the front desk, ask them. For a second, I feel even more pathetic. I'm like an old man with dementia. I'm lucky I don't need help wiping my ass.

The outside is so much different than I pictured.

The closer I got to my parole hearing, the more convinced I was that there would be some kind of process. A sort of easing into things for the post-release inmate. When I mentioned it to my C.O., motherfucker laughed at me and handed me a booklet. The morning of my release, he handed me some cash—my total earnings. Twenty years of pennies on the hour, and I can't even afford a second night at a shithole motel.

I need to make that call, because it's the only chance I have.

Otherwise, I'll be right back in within hours of walking out.

Sucking in a breath between my teeth, I pick up the phone again and call the front desk.

A chipper female voice answers—a young voice. "Days Inn front desk. How can I help you?"

"Hey there, sweetheart," I drawl. My voice is smoked whiskey, smooth but with a bite. "I need to look someone up in Connecticut."

She draws in a breath, then hesitates. "You're serious?" Her voice lilts, amused.

I lay it on thick, dropping my voice several octaves—still sweet, but low enough to drop panties. "Yeah, baby. I really need your help."

A giggle caresses my ear before she can collect herself. She's definitely young.

I close my eyes for a moment, the memory of another small laugh pricking at me. The anger rises up quickly, fire shooting through my veins. I struggle to stuff it down, to shove the lid on it before it can backdraft, blowing me straight out of the room and right back into Lewisburg Pen.

"What's the name?" she asks, completely oblivious to the man burning on the other end.

Sucking in a deep breath, I manage to slow it for a moment. "Lucy Demmel." Saying her name only makes it worse. The panic shoves its way in. I wonder if she's even alive. If she's healthy. Safe. Or if she's just another statistic, too. I jump up from the bed. Pace the room. Wait.

The receptionist spells out our last name, and the sound of tapping reaches my ears. It's a weird tapping, though—a computer keyboard.

I frown. "Aren't you going to patch me through?"

She laughs. "I'm looking her up on Facebook. Hold on."

My eyebrows furrow. Facebook? Before I can ask what the fuck that is, my angel lets out a triumphant "Ah-ha!" and rattles off a number to me. I fumble for the pen and notepad in the drawer, ask her to repeat it, and jot it down.

"Are you sure that's really her?" I need to know, because I can't take the disappointment.

"Lucy Demmel," she says, as if she's reading. "Twenty-eight, lives in Naugatuck, Connecticut. Went to Naugatuck High School. She's in a relationship—"

"Wait." I take another deep breath. "How do you know all

this?" The age is right. The town, too. "Never mind," I say, even as my angel laughs at me. Flat out laughs. Not just amused. She's almost hysterical. "How does she look?"

The laughter dies. "You're not, like, a stalker . . . are you?"

I sigh. "She's my cousin. Same last name. Come on. What does she look like?"

She makes a skeptical sound, like a *hmph*. "Maybe I shouldn't have given you her number. Oh shit. Am I going to get fired? Please don't get me fired. I can't keep a job—"

Christ. I've always been a magnet for headaches. "Shh, baby. I'm not a stalker. She really is my cousin. Check my room records. My last name is Demmel. But don't call me Clifford, or I'll . . ." The threat dies on my lips, because it's not an idle one. I blink, and wonder how long it'll take for the prison effect to wear off. How long before I'm normal again. I don't even know who I am anymore, or what normal is.

"She has long red hair. Kinda wavy, like. Real sad green eyes. And . . ." Her pause stretches, almost endless. "A beauty mark or mole thing right near her eyebrow."

I almost cry with relief. That's my Lucy.

"Her last post: 'Strength isn't keeping your tears locked up when you're sad, it's saying no to a marriage proposal from the sexiest, sweetest man alive, even when everyone expects you to say yes. Fuck that shit.'" She snorts. "*What*?" She whisper-reads it again.

That fucked up sense of humor is Lucy, all the way. I rattle off the phone number back at my angel to make sure I got it right, then hang up.

I pick up the phone again and dial the number. It rings, the connection crackly but real. I almost lose my shit. I don't know what I'm going to say. Or if she even remembers me. She was so little. Maybe she blocked the whole thing out.

A loud male voice booms into my ear. "PLEASE DIAL THE

NUMERAL ONE BEFORE THE AREA CODE. This is a recording."

I hang up, muttering a "No shit." Clearing my throat, I try again—this time dialing one. I vaguely remember needing to do that before I went in.

This time, the call goes through. It rings five times, and then my heart stops.

"Hey, you've reached Lucy. You know what to do, dontcha?"

The disappointment shoots into me. My shoulders slump and I almost drop the phone onto the floor.

"Please leave a message after the tone. When you are finished recording, hang up, or press one for more options."

A shrill *beep* pierces my ears, and I nearly drop the phone again.

"Shit. No, wait. Sorry, Luce." I pause. Suddenly I really have no idea what to say. "Uh, yeah. Luce, this is Cliff. I don't know if you remember me. It's been ages since I got a letter from you. I assumed your parents shut that shit down real fast. Sorry. Well, I guess you're not eight anymore, so it's okay to swear around you."

I'm babbling. Taking a deep breath, I try to make words that won't freak her out.

"Luce, I know this is asking a lot. And do you even go by Luce anymore? Or do you prefer Lucy?" I rake my free hand through my hair. I'm fucking this up. Majorly. I let out a low, frustrated sound. "Okay, look, I'm at the Days Inn in Lewisburg. Fucking Pennsylvania, Luce. I'm just gonna lay it all out here: I have no money, nowhere to go, and I have to stick around at least long enough to see my parole officer. So maybe . . ."

Suddenly I realize how desperate I sound. But I *am*.

"Sorry to bother you, Luce—*Lucy*. Just forget it."

I hang up.

Dressing, I decide I'm better off spending my time finding a job. If I'm going to get out of this ass crack of a town, I'm gonna need cash—fast. There's got to be a diner or something looking for suckers who don't mind bussing tables for minimum wage. And maybe they'll even overlook my record.

The odds of me finding a job are even lower than finding Lucy. I figure my angel at the front desk can't possibly save me twice, but maybe she can. Maybe she's from around here and knows of a place that will hire without asking questions. Or she can at least point me to the closest drug dealer so I can start selling too.

I really will be a statistic if I don't get my shit together.

My hand is on the door knob when the phone rings. I freeze, then turn in slow motion toward the nightstand where the phone rests. But it keeps ringing, and I have to accept that I'm not imagining it.

I dart across the room and grab it, pressing it to my ear. "Yeah. Lucy?"

"Cliff," she sobs. "Is it really you?"

A relieved sigh escapes my lips. "It's me," I say with a smile. She sounds so different, yet I'd know that voice anywhere.

"You're really out? I can't believe it. I thought you had another five years."

"Yeah, I got lucky. Overcrowding and good behavior." Mostly. Plus I had a lawyer that was really good at talking judges into dreamland.

"Cliff, holy shit. Where are you? I mean, I *know* where, but when are you coming home?" She's talking so fast, I can barely understand her. I love every second of it.

I hate to disappoint her. Even after all these years. "Luce . . ."

I can almost hear her shoulders slump. "You're not coming home?"

"Not likely. At least, not anytime soon. I'm broke, kid. And I—"

"I'll PayPal you some money," she says, and now she's really talking fast. I strain to understand her, the words like a foreign language. At least her accent is Connecticut.

I let her finish, again wishing I had a cigarette. Something to calm my nerves.

"Cliff? You there?"

Swallowing past the dry lump in my throat, I tell her I am. "I've got no clue what you're talking about, Luce."

"Okay, just give me your email address."

She's going to think I'm an alien, that the games we played when she was a kid were real. "I don't have one."

She barks out a laugh. "What? Oh. No Wi-Fi in prison."

"Wi-Fi?" My head starts to throb.

"Um . . . Like AOL, but wireless." She laughs again. "Wow, this is so funny. You're like a newborn."

It's good that she can be so positive about this—about anything.

"All right, let me think." She hums a little. "No email address, and I'm guessing you don't have a bank account either. Jesus, prison is inhumane. Well, there's only one solution."

I shrug, because seeing as how I can barely grasp this Wi-Fi stuff, I'm probably going to be blown away by whatever she comes up with.

"Cliff, text me your address."

The throbbing between my eyes intensifies. "Luce, I don't—"

"Fuck," she yells. "You probably don't even know what a cell phone is."

"I know what a cell phone is," I shoot back.

"Yeah, the clunky TV-remote-looking ones from the early 2000s," she jokes.

Both of my eyebrows lift. "Everything is different now, huh?" My voice is low, but not that flirtatious purr I used on the girl at the front desk. I sound sad. I need to man the fuck up.

"It is," she agrees. "But don't worry. I'm gonna take care of you, reintroduce you to the wild. And teach you how to play Pokémon GO."

"I know how to play Pokémon," I grumble.

She laughs again. "This is way different, trust me. It uses GPS and—"

"Okay, mercy. My head hurts."

Her giggle, however, is a soothing mother's stroke across my forehead. It reminds me of better times. "I'm gonna come down there, okay?"

"You don't have to do that," I tell her. I'm supposed to be a man. It should be *me* taking care of her, not the other way around.

She snorts. "Dude," she says, "trust me. You need a guide. And I'm currently on vacation, licking my wounds."

I suddenly remember what the receptionist read to me. "You got married?"

"No," she says, almost sadly. "It's against my rules."

"What are you, a nun?" For a second, it feels like I've gone back twenty years in time, like we're just kids busting each other's balls.

"Nuns," she says, "don't have one-night stands."

I nearly choke. "I don't ever want to know about your sex life."

"You sure? You don't want to live vicariously? Must've been awfully lonely in prison." I can practically hear her smirking.

"No," I tell her firmly. A few seconds pass. My voice softens. "Hey, Luce? Thanks."

Her voice is so small when she finally responds. "No, Cliff, thank *you*."

I shake my head, wondering if other people have these kinds of conversations. Sighing, I let her direct the conversation for a few. She rattles off times and schedules, then promises to be at my room before checkout time.

"Please set a wakeup call," she begs.

"Yeah, yeah." I smile, though. "Hey, Luce? What's Facebook?"

2

OLIVIA

"**A**re you sure you want to do this?" my sister Lucy asks me for the thousandth time. She lifts a man's shirt on its hanger from a rack and examines the price tag. It's one of those super soft henley shirts—the ones that belong on Calvin Klein models but look good on anyone.

I peg her with my best baby sister look, the wide-eyed "Please play Barbies with me" one. Works every time. She sighs, shaking her head.

"You're going to miss class, Livvie. And I don't know how long this is going to take." It's a half-hearted attempt. She tucks a curl behind her ear and tilts her head.

"It's like a free vacation," I tell her, grabbing the cart she's pushing and leading it toward a table of men's jeans. "Is he a bootcut kind of guy, do you think?"

Lucy frowns, a crease forming between her eyebrows. "I'm not sure. And Pennsylvania is cold this time of year. It's really not like a vacation, kid."

Even though we're both in our twenties, Lucy is seven years older than me. Sometimes it feels like an eternity—especially when I was still into Barbies and she was experimenting with makeup. She'll be thirty before I hit twenty-five, which is usually prime marriage age, but not for Lucy. She'll never get married.

"Well," I say, drawing out the word, "it will be, if he's hot."

Lucy nearly chokes. Her face streaks through with red, and the tips of her ears practically glow. "He's like your cousin," she hisses.

I think of all the ways our parents will disapprove of this, how they already disapprove of him. This morning, when Lucy filled me in on what she was doing, she made me promise not to tell Mom and Dad. I'm twenty-one and yet apparently still have to swear to little sister secrecy. Other than that, she didn't tell me much. Just that our cousin Cliff needed some help because he just got out of prison. And then those cherry red lips of hers clamped shut.

It's weird, because Lucy and I tell each other everything. Seven years is a lucky number. We were meant to be.

"Dude, I'm dying to know. What did he go away for?" I start unfolding jeans, checking sizes and seeing how they fall. I've never dressed a guy before. It's kind of turning me on, and I haven't even met him yet. I don't know what to expect, so I imagine that he's tall and muscular, with dark eyes and long hair. A beard, for sure. And he's *broad*. He could throw me around in bed like a rag doll. I smirk.

"Stop that," Lucy hisses. She throws me a glare.

I sigh. The past three years of college were fun, but this new semester has me in a bit of a dry spell. Everyone is focusing on their GPAs, which is odd considering we're all legal drinking age now. You'd think they'd all be at the bar with me. Not that I don't want to graduate and get a good job. But this is it, the last semester before we're shoved into adulthood. Real responsibility and all that. Not only am I curious about the ex-con, but I'm also bored. And when I get bored . . .

"Please try not to get into trouble," Lucy continues, reading my mind. It's her superpower. "Mom and Dad will kill me if they find out I dragged you into this."

"Dragged me into what?" I toss several pairs of jeans into the cart, then face her. Crossing my arms, I give her another baby sis look. It's almost too easy—usually, anyway.

But this time, Lucy ignores me. She takes back control of the cart and marches toward the checkout queue. Frowning, I follow her, grabbing a makeup palette off a shelf as I pass it and chucking it into the cart. She owes me, damn it.

"We've got to catch our train," Lucy reminds me again over her shoulder as she piles everything onto the checkout counter. "So no time for smoke breaks, understand?"

It's like I'm seven again and our parents let us go to the mall alone for the first time. I hold my hands up, backing away. "All right. If you've got this, then, I'm going outside." There's no way I'm getting into a car with her for forty-five minutes and then hopping on a train for twelve billion hours without a cigarette first.

Outside, the icy air blasts into me and I huddle deep into my coat. Cupping the flame, I light the cigarette, wishing it could warm me up. A gust of wind whips around the corner of the building, and I turn, shivering.

Maybe this whole thing is a bad idea. Lucy is right—I would be missing classes. Call it a case of senior-itis, but I'm desperate to stretch my wings. I need a break from the monotony of sleep-class-food-class. And I'll be honest: Lucy got my curiosity going. As I smoke, I run back through the tidbits she's given me. I know his name, that he just got out of prison in Pennsylvania, and that Lucy was the only one he could call. I guess he must be the black sheep of the family—maybe got busted for drugs. It is kind of weird that he wasn't serving in Connecticut, though.

I suck the cigarette down, toss it into the parking lot, and nearly crash into Lucy as she comes through the doors.

"Shit, sorry." I touch her arms to steady her.

"Cold?" she asks with a smirk.

We throw ourselves into the car, the heater on blast but not nearly hot enough. Lucy makes a barely livable wage as a teacher. Her car is a decade old and sometimes the warm air coming out of the vents smells like burning rubber. She also has to get out and slam her fist into the left headlight to get it to work.

But she has a car, which is more than I've got.

We drive to the train station in New Haven, and I say a silent prayer that it isn't the one with no walls or anything. It's way too cold for that shit. But as we pull into the Union Avenue parking lot, relief washes through me. It's the bigger one, the one with heat and bathrooms. Not that we have time to even enjoy it, according to Lucy. You'd think the world was going to end if we missed this train.

Lucy parks, and I wonder if it's safe to leave her car unattended in New Haven for a week plus. It might be a lemon but it's all she's got. But there is a gate and a guy sitting in the booth, so I try to convince myself that no one will jack it. Older cars are a lot easier to steal. All they'd have to do is pay the parking fee.

"How much is this gonna cost you?" I ask as she hauls our suitcases out of the trunk. She plunks mine down in front of me, then hands me the shopping bags full of Cliff's new clothes. I'm not at all surprised that she's doing all this, though. Lucy may be afraid of commitment, but when it comes to people she loves, she'd give you the shirt off your back. Still, it's kind of odd that she's never mentioned Cliff before if she used to be so close with him.

Lucy shrugs. "It doesn't matter."

Eyes narrowing, I scrutinize her face. It's hard to tell in the dim lighting of the parking lot, but she looks funny. I can't put a name to her expression, though. She almost looks pained, but happy—like she just got a bullet in the leg but told she won the lottery right after.

I follow her, frowning at her back. She's acting so weird. And

I'm not used to there being secrets between us. I resolve to flirt the truth out of Cliff the second I'm alone with him. He may be my cousin, but there's nothing wrong with a little flirting.

"This way," Lucy says, pushing through the entrance. Wishing I'd smoked one last cigarette during the walk over, I hurry after her. The station doesn't look at all like I'd pictured it. I bite my lip, realizing that I've never been on a train. Or a plane. I'm like a travel virgin.

"What if I have to pee?" I chase her to the departure list. It flips, a loud clacking sound echoing through the lobby.

My sister studies the times, nodding to herself. "It's not that bad. You'll get used to it."

"So there *is* a bathroom on this thing?"

She takes off again, heading toward our track. I have no idea how any of this works. With my luck, I'd get on the wrong one if I had to do this alone. There aren't even people to ask, unless you want to go all the way back to the front desk or find someone at a track. This whole thing is totally DIY, and I don't like it. It's too much of a reminder that in three months, I'll be doing all of it myself, every day.

"Status is 'Boarding,' so hurry!" Lucy breaks into a brisk walk-jog thing. Groaning, I step up my pace.

We run through a freezing cold tunnel that's connected to the rest of the station by a wide open archway. The state must pay an arm and a leg to keep the rest of the place warm. The air smells heavy with body odor, exhaust, and cigarette smoke. My fingers twitch toward the pack in my coat pocket, but Lucy glances back at me, a fierce glare on her face. I run faster.

Finally we reach our train. She leads me onto it, and my legs shake with gratitude for the seat I'm about to plop into. But every single row is full.

Gaping, I turn toward her. "We're not that late!"

She smiles a little, shaking her head. "Come on."

Lucy leads me toward a door on an end of the car. Then she

disappears into it, lugging her rolling suitcase behind her. I dart after her, and find myself in a small connecting tunnel, encased from the elements with heavy vinyl flaps. Through the window in the door of the next car, I see Lucy plowing forward. Every seat in that car is full, too.

Glancing down, I'm shocked to see a flash of the track, lit by the lights of the train station. I hope I won't have to walk through one of these once we're moving, then hurry to catch up.

Eventually we find a pair of empty seats. Lucy shoves her luggage into a compartment above our heads and I mimic her like a good little sister. Then we collapse.

The seats are surprisingly comfortable. I snuggle into mine and wiggle my toes in my boots. Then I peer around our car.

The whole thing is full. There are still people wandering the cars, looking for a place to sit. The train starts to move, and everyone who is walking grabs onto something to steady themselves as they continue their trek. I'm super grateful that we found seats at all, never mind two together. Looking around, though, I start to worry that I really will have to walk between cars to pee.

"Uh, Luce?" I turn toward her.

She stares out the window, her brown hair a veil around her face. "Hmn?"

"Where's the bathroom?"

Lucy shifts in her seat. A soft smile plays on her lips. "At the back of the car. If you have to pee, I'd go now. It gets pretty rank after about six hours."

I glance back and notice the door on the left. "Won't it stink up the whole car?"

She shakes her head. "There's like a squirt of Febreze every so often coming through the air vents. Plus we're far enough away from the door. This is the best spot, trust me."

"I'll deal with anything as long as I don't have to hop cars while we're moving," I tell her.

"Why do you think I hunted for seats?" she asks with a grin.

I start to tell her it's pretty obvious, since they were all taken, but instead I smile back. Truth be told, I'm nervous about spending half a day on a train—overnight. Adjusting to the dorms at school was cake compared to this. I don't know how I'll sleep or where I'll get coffee in the morning.

Reading my mind again, Lucy pats the purse balanced on her knees. It's more like a tote bag. "I've got Starbucks fraps in here. They'll be room temp by morning but they'll do the trick."

"Have I told you lately that I love you?" I quick-hug her by resting my head on her shoulder for a second, pressing our arms together.

Lucy exhales, a long breath. For a second, guilt flickers in her eyes. Then she smiles, and like the sun after a storm, all of the clouds scatter. "I love you too, Livvie."

My gut twists. This trip is not going to end well. I just know it.

MORNING RISES and my eyes feel like sandpaper. Just as I'd thought, I didn't sleep. It's impossible to drift off when you're rocking and jolting over bumps. Lucy didn't sleep either, so I don't feel too bad. We can be miserable together.

But my sister is anything but miserable as the train lurches into the Amtrak station. She's practically chipper as she gets our luggage down from their compartment and practically skips toward the exit. I shamble after her, reminding myself that at least we're here.

"Hey, how did you get time off anyway?" I ask her as we step off the train and into fresh air. I step to the side, letting go of my suitcase long enough to light a cigarette.

"Toss it," she instructs in her teacher voice.

I lift an eyebrow at her while taking a nice, long drag. There's nothing like a first cigarette after hours of deprivation.

"Our ride is here."

Rolling my eyes, I point the cigarette at her. "It can wait. It's not like we have far to go."

Lucy presses her lips together and smiles guiltily, eyebrows lifted.

"We *don't* have far to go . . . right?"

With a shrug, she grabs her suitcase and heads toward an Escalade idling in the parking lot. "We're in Harrisburg, about an hour away from Lewisburg."

My shoulders slump. Smoking as quickly as possible, I chase her to the Escalade. She must've called an Uber. I pray that the driver doesn't have a non-smoking policy, but the dirty look he gives me as we near pops my little bubble. Taking one last drag, I toss it onto the pavement.

The closer we get to Lewisburg, the more keyed up I feel. Lucy had the driver stop at a Starbucks, so I feel slightly more human now. Curiosity is what's really fueling me. Using a compact mirror, I touch up the makeup that was smudged by our harrowing overnight train ride and smooth my hair. Lucy raises an eyebrow at me but says nothing, and the driver lets us pick songs from his iPod. Not a bad deal, considering he made me waste my cigarette.

And then suddenly we're in Lewisburg, and the Escalade pulls up in front of the entrance to a Days Inn. A man paces out front, his hands shoved into the pockets of his coat. Long brown hair that's nearly black frames his face, and he's got a beard, so I can't really make out his features. But he's *big*.

Not in a heavy way. He's tall and broad. Even with that bulky hand-me-down coat, I can tell he's built. It's like I'm psychic and imagined him into being. Biting my lip, I stifle a giggle. For all I know, he's really ugly and has a beer gut.

It really *has* been too long since I've gotten laid.

Lucy pays the Uber guy, we grab our luggage, and then my sister and I are standing in front of the motel with Cliff.

"They kicked you out?" she asks him.

He looks up, and depthless brown eyes meet hers. Despite the massive amounts of fur on his face, he's handsome.

Hot, even.

There's a scar next to his eyebrow that's more like a pocked hole. It looks like someone bludgeoned him with a big rock. They probably did. But the rest of his face is intact—no teardrop tattoos or anything like that. His eyes are surprisingly soft and kind. When he smiles at Lucy, it lights up his whole face.

I decide he definitely went to jail for selling drugs, and wonder how long before he's connected again. I could use some bud.

"Checkout was eleven," he says with a shrug. He peers at her, almost timidly. "You look good, kid."

Kid? I blink. Squinting, I examine him more closely. I note the lines at the corners of his eyes and the dark circles beneath them. He's got to be in his early thirties, maybe older. I pluck my pack of cigarettes from my pocket and light one, exhaling smoke into the air.

"Olivia," Lucy says, exasperated. She gestures toward the motel entrance, as if someone is going to walk out into my cloud of smoke any second. The parking lot is close to empty, the place desolate.

"Yeah, *Olivia*," Cliff says, eyebrows lifted. "Sharing is caring." He holds his hand out for one.

A grin spreads across my face. Resisting the urge to stick my tongue out at my sister, I hand him the pack and my lighter.

He lights up, and his entire face relaxes as if I just took his cock into my mouth instead of sharing a cigarette. Putting my own cigarette between my lips, I stuff down the giggle that is bubbling up. I really *am* sleep deprived.

"Been a while?" I ask when I get myself under control. Even that statement is dangerously close to twelve-year-old humor. I take another drag.

Cliff nods and smokes thoughtfully for a minute. His eyes never leave mine. They're a deep brown, but so warm—like redwood. "It's been twenty years since I had a cigarette that wasn't stale. But that's not all I've been missing." He grins, a devilish smirk that shoots straight to my lower abdomen. The implication behind his words might be in my head.

Lucy clears her throat loudly. "Clifford, this is Olivia, my little sister."

The color drains from his face and he chokes on his cigarette. "Sister?" he sputters.

I snort. "Relax," I tell him with a wink. "I'm adopted."

3

CLIFF

It's been just about twenty-four hours since I got out, and only one thing is very clear: Lucy isn't happy with me.

Sitting in the coffee shop, I'm very careful to not make eye contact with Olivia or say anything that might be mistaken as flirting. My cousin is full of plans, telling me how she spent the entire train ride researching parole and all that. Since remaining in the state of Pennsylvania isn't a condition of my release, Lucy thinks we can get me transferred to a P.O. in Connecticut.

All I can think about, though, is how I've already disappointed her. I had no idea that Olivia was her sister. My cousin, I guess. They're seven years apart, which makes her seventeen years younger than me. An entire lifetime, basically. My head is spinning with everything.

"Let's set up your phone," Lucy says, scooting closer to me.

I pull the phone out of my pocket. It's one of her old ones, but completely new to me. Instead of plastic, the screen is glass, and there are almost no buttons. You can send written messages on it or play video games. There are these things called "apps" that allow you to do different things—even video chat. Lucy explains all of this to me again, showing me how to text and FaceTime her.

She also downloads an app called Uber and tells me that I'll never need to call for a taxi again. Then she downloads Facebook.

"Let's get you signed up," she says, her eyes intent on the screen.

Standing up, I leave her to it and amble toward the counter. I need gallons of coffee today. For one, it's been aeons since I've had coffee that didn't taste like water or mud. No in-between in prison. But really, I didn't sleep a wink last night. I kept waking up to every little sound, shooting straight up in bed with my fists cocked anytime someone walked past my door.

Old habits die hard.

I order another venti something or other and step to the side while the barista makes it.

"Luce gets kinda batty when she's nervous," Olivia says from my elbow.

Literally. I tower over her.

Turning, I glance down at her and nod. "She's been really helpful. Too helpful." I shove my hands into the pockets of my brand-new Levis, feeling more than a little guilty. The thermal henley is snug but hugs every muscle in my arms and abs, and the color is right, too.

Black.

Always black.

I'll never wear orange or tan again.

"Looks good on you," Olivia says, her eyes roving over me.

Those eyes.

When I was a kid, I had the biggest crush on Christina Ricci in *Casper*. Olivia's eyes are just as mesmerizing. A brown so warm, they're almost liquid. She's got what they'd call soulful eyes.

Then there are the dimples that pop up every time she smiles. Sweet, yet mischievous. Alluring, like a single beauty mark. Like the dark curls that cascade over her arms. There's a wildness to her but also a softness, as if she's straddling heaven and hell.

I'd like for her to straddle *me*.

I swallow hard. Lucy may not be happy about it, but let's get real. Olivia is the first woman I've been near in the last twenty years. I realize that she was a year old when I went in, and I look away. She's too young. And she's basically family. She is off limits. I'll probably need to tell myself this every five minutes—especially once the three of us are sharing the same motel room. In some ways, this is worse than being in seg.

"So," Olivia says, and I swear she's inching closer to me.

I lift my eyebrows at her in what I hope is a "go away, kid, you bother me" look. Seventeen years between us. Twenty-one years old. Too young. *Family.*

She smirks back at me as if she can read my thoughts. Or she's fucking with me. "Luce didn't really say much about you."

I stiffen, because I know what's coming: the big question. Olivia doesn't know yet, and I'd rather keep it that way. I'm going to need all the friends I can muster. That was in the brochure: a solid support system. At the time, it made me roll my eyes, but now it's my only mission.

Friends. Job. Head down.

I eye Olivia suspiciously, but she doesn't look away.

"Got any tattoos?" she asks, eyes dancing. Those eyes could kill a man. They're round and innocent at first glance, but the more I look at her, the more expressive her eyes are. Paired with the dark curls that cascade down her back, and she is man's ruin.

And I should not be looking at her.

"Nope." The barista hands me my coffee and I give her a grateful nod. I glance over at the table we were sitting at, but Lucy still has her face in my phone. I look quickly at Olivia, then back at my coffee. "You?"

"You'd think someone who, you know, would have a lot of tattoos." An eyebrow arches. She's definitely fucking with me.

"I was eighteen when I went in," I say quietly.

She motions to the door and wiggles her pack of cigarettes in my face. Sooner or later, I'm going to have to beg one of these women to buy me my own pack. I nod and follow her out. We both light up and she steps back, regarding me with too much curiosity.

"How old are you now?" she asks, voice soft. Compassionate, even. She's not being judgmental. Those eyes are wider than usual, and her lips are pressed together. Like she's wondering how much she needs to tell me about the world. She's put two and two together fast, since Lucy had to tell me what Uber is.

I smoke my cigarette and take a swig of coffee to buy myself some time. Because the second I tell her how long it's been, she'll know that what I did was bad. And then we probably won't be friends. I won't tell her, I decide. If Lucy didn't want to tell her, I shouldn't, either. "It doesn't matter," I say. "We're cousins, remember?"

"Yes," she says slowly, as if she's speaking to someone who is either being obtuse or hasn't had enough coffee yet. And maybe I haven't. "So dontcha think we should share things with each other?" She looks pointedly at the cigarette in my hand.

This woman.

"Look," she says, "Lucy might tell you otherwise, but I'm not a baby. I've been drinking and fucking for years now. I think I can handle a little honesty."

I drop my cigarette and stub it out with my boot. "It's not my story to tell." I stride toward the door, suddenly eager to get back to my iPhone lesson. But as I pull the door open, I hear a little snort of doubtful laughter from behind me, and now I know two things.

Lucy isn't happy with me, and Olivia has got my number.

~

"YOU HAVE SO MUCH CATCHING up to do," Lucy tells me. We're camped out in our shared motel room with two doubles: one for the ladies, and the other for the ex-con. We're supposed to be going out to dinner, but my cousin can't decide where to take me. "I mean, you don't even know what a Crunchwrap is. Did you ever have sushi before you went in?"

I glance at the bathroom door. Olivia is getting ready, but I have no idea how much she can hear. "Luce," I whisper, "how much does she know?" I nod toward the bathroom.

Her face pales, and I instantly regret asking.

I hold up my hands. "I haven't told her anything. It's not my place."

Eyebrows knitting together, she shakes her head. "It's totally up to you."

We haven't really had a chance to talk about this. I'm not even sure she remembers what went down. For all I know, she just remembers taking turns playing Crash Bandicoot in my parents' living room. Maybe she just remembers how much she loved her big cousin Cliff, and none of the bad things. This only makes me feel guiltier.

"Luce, we really need to—"

The bathroom door opens and Olivia steps out. Everything I was going to say evaporates.

Despite the low temperatures outside, she's wearing a sweater dress that falls only to her knees. No tights or pantyhose. Bare thigh disappears into knee-high boots. Lucy clears her throat and I realize I'm staring.

"Boom, baby," Olivia says, turning around in a circle. She points to the makeup around her eyes. It's smoky and understated, but so fucking sexy. With a wink to Lucy, she says, "Thank you for the palette, by the way."

My cousin sighs and gestures to the jeans and sweater she's wearing. "Livvie, we're just going to Taco Bell." She looks at me. "I mean, unless there's something you're really jonesing for."

In the twenty years I was inside, I rarely thought about the food I missed. My mom wasn't much of a cook, and whenever I thought of the delicious things my grandmother used to make, I felt nauseous. So I learned to stop thinking about it, and to appreciate the gray-colored slop on my tray. Because, all things considered, it wasn't that bad—unless you were in seg. There was no way to pretend those loaves were food.

I shrug and give Lucy a smile. "I'm actually kind of pumped for the Demmel Fast Food Reunion Tour."

Her smile is so big, her eyes go all squinty. For a second, she's eight again and I've let her win at Pokémon cards. "I've missed you, Cliff."

There's no hint of fear in her eyes. Just admiration. I don't know what to think. Maybe she really doesn't remember. "Yeah, you too, kid." I stand from my bed and spread my arms. "All right, ladies. Lead the way."

Lucy calls another Uber and I make a mental note to ask her how this is less expensive than renting a car. Someday, I promise myself, I'm going to pay her back for all of this. I don't know how yet, but I will.

The driver takes us through several drive-thrus: Taco Bell, McDonald's, and a Papa John's. I'm really suspicious about fast food pizza—which I managed to avoid before I went in—but Olivia gives me eyes that plead with me not to burst Lucy's bubble.

I would do anything, with those eyes asking.

We take all of our food back to the motel room, and suddenly Olivia's dress makes a lot of sense. She puts away more food than I could ever eat in one sitting and, as she reminds us, she doesn't have to unbutton her jeans because she's not wearing any. Lucy only eats half a cheeseburger, though.

When Olivia and I go onto the balcony for our after dinner smoke, I forget that I'm kind of nervous to be alone with her—for multiple reasons.

"What's up with Lucy?" I ask.

She hugs herself against the cold. I was all for breaking the non-smoking room rule, but she insisted that we go out. "I've been wondering the same thing," she says.

I'm taken aback by her honesty. Most women would just shrug and pretend not to know. "So this really isn't her."

Leaning against the railing, Olivia shakes her head. "Ever since she told me she was coming to see you."

So Lucy does remember. She must. "Did she say why she wanted to come?" I need to know whether she pities me or is afraid of me.

"Lucy doesn't usually explain her choices to us peons." Olivia sighs. "Honestly, I don't know what's going on with her. We usually tell each other everything." She pins me with one of her looks. "I was hoping you might give me some insight."

If I don't tell her, the brain behind those eyes is going to be on overdrive trying to figure it out. I can already sense that Olivia isn't the kind of person who is satisfied with the status quo. And it's been clear that she sees straight through anyone's bullshit. Even mine. Our eyes meet, and I hold her gaze. Trying to decide. To tell, or not.

Her eyes narrow. A dimple appears in her cheek. "I bet you got put away because Lucy jacked a car and you took the fall."

At least, I hope so. "Nothing like that," I tell her.

"So no car-jacking?" She leans close, and I can smell her perfume. It's a warm mix of vanilla and sandalwood, maybe even some jasmine. Her lips are only inches from mine. All I have to do is duck down, sweep her into my arms, and—

The sliding glass door rolls open and Lucy steps out onto the balcony with us. We separate like smoke, and I return my attention to locking lips with my cigarette.

Lucy waves her phone in the air. "I just got an email from your probation officer. He said he'll submit the form for your request." She grins, bouncing on the balls of her feet a little. "You can come home. Maybe even in a couple days!"

"That's great, Luce. Thank you." I wrap an arm around her.

"For everything." I press a kiss to the side of her head and she nuzzles in. I would do anything for this woman, and it's still not enough. It never will be.

"So now we need to talk about where you're going to stay," she says, ducking out of my embrace. She bounces back toward the door. "Inside, where it's warm." She waves for us to hurry, then slips back into the warmth of the room.

Olivia snubs out her cigarette and tilts her head back to look up at me. "I'd say you can stay with me," she says with a smirk, "but I have to share my apartment with another girl. We even get undressed in front of each other."

When she sweeps past me, she presses her ass into my thigh. Then she disappears inside. When I glance down at my cigarette, I realize it went out minutes ago.

I THOUGHT LEAVING Lewisburg was going to be the hardest part, but Lucy seized that little problem by the reins. It took almost a week, but our request was approved. My new P.O. insisted we meet the second I set foot back in Connecticut—a relatively simple condition, considering I thought I'd never go home again.

Home.

I'm not even sure Naugatuck is home anymore. I have no family left, other than Lucy. I guess Olivia, too, though we have different last names. Her name is Reynolds, and it suits her. It's a German surname, meaning "to rule." If that isn't Olivia, I don't know what is.

If Lucy took over my case, Olivia has consumed my thoughts. Though I no longer jump at every single sound during the night, I'm wide awake thinking about her. I replay bits of conversation we shared during the day. I trace her face onto the velvety under-side of my eyes. And sometimes I even dream about her.

I'm ashamed to admit it, but this week I've already had three dirty dreams starring Olivia Reynolds. Living in a motel room with two women has made it really hard to be a man. The only alone time I get is when I'm shitting or showering. I've jerked off more times than I can count, and I'm pretty sure both of them think I have an odd fixation on cleanliness. So far, neither of them have noticed my extracurricular activities. But if I don't get back in the game soon, it's going to get a lot harder.

In more than one way.

Obviously it can't be Olivia. I've already resolved to stay away from her, and she's too close to me anyway. It has to be a one-night stand, with a woman I'll never see again. Lewisburg is a good choice, considering Pennsylvania is several states away from home and, in a few more days, I'll be gone forever. But I can't figure out how to meet any women around here.

Though drinking isn't against the terms of my parole, there's no way I'll be able to go to a bar alone. Neither of them mean to be helicopters, but these two are almost worse than the C.O.s in prison. Plus, I don't have a dollar to my name. It seems kind of wrong to ask to borrow money and then tell Lucy she can't come with me. And since they've been feeding me and attending to every single one of my needs, there's really no excuse for me to go anywhere on my own.

At least not until it's time to meet with my Lewisburg probation officer.

It's more of a formality, since I'm transferring, but it gives me the out I need. I tell Lucy and Olivia that I don't know how long it'll take, then walk to the office. It's cold as fuck, but walking keeps me warm and gives me time to think. One of the conditions of my parole is finding a full-time job within thirty days or at least enrolling in a full-time continuing education program. I'd already graduated high school when I went in—with a pretty sweet GPA—so I could go to college if I wanted to.

But I'm already so much older than the kids taking English 101. If I matriculated now, I'd be almost forty-three by the time I graduate. And I don't even know what I'd study. All of my pre-penitentiary hopes and dreams seem silly now. No one is going to hire a felon like me, even with an undergraduate degree.

The Department of Social Services office looks like every other government building: squat, yellow-gray, and brick. I stroll through the doors and give my name to the security guard. I'm waved through and led to a small windowless office with a grubby gray carpet. Bright florescent lights press down on me. A mustached P.O. with a bald head and deep brown skin sits across from me behind a desk and holds out his hand for me to shake. His hair is as gray as the floor, and the bags under his eyes suggest he's probably not very alert.

The name sewn on his uniform is Ntshiza.

"How you doing, man?" I greet him.

He nods, long and slow. "How are *you*?" His voice is deep and gravelly, as tired as he looks.

I wonder if he's tired because he dedicates himself to his clients. I decide to try and find out. "Lousy," I tell him. "I can't sleep and I'm freaked out. My cousin is picking out my clothes and I need to get laid."

Ntshiza laughs. "Aren't you a breath of fresh air." He settles back in his seat. "Okay, son. You're only here for a little longer, so there's not much I can do for you."

I sit forward. "Yeah. I got the email that my request was approved."

He gives me another slow series of nods. Reaching into a desk drawer, he pulls out a pack of cigarettes. He lights up and then slides them to me, touching a finger to his nose and lips like Santa Claus. "You have to see your new probation officer in three days, understand?" The smoke curls from his mouth, drifting into the air.

I nod. "I won't fuck this up."

"For your sake, I hope not." He regards me with solemn brown eyes. There's warmth in them, too, though. "Demmel, you're not a bad guy."

I exhale smoke toward the ceiling. "Do you tell all of your guys that?"

Ntshiza shakes his head. "Just the ones I believe in. Listen, your new P.O. is a friend of mine. We go way back. He'll go easy on you and he'll help you, if you let him. Got it?"

I nod again, feeling like a little kid in the principal's office. Ntshiza is the first person in a position of power in the last twenty years to really give a shit about me. I probably should take what he's saying with a grain of salt, but it feels so fucking good to have someone on my side, even if he's an old and tired P.O.

"He's got a job lined up for you."

I sit up straighter. "Really?" I wonder what it is. Maybe the job is really terrible. Still, I want to hope.

"Your file mentioned that you got into quite a few fights during your sentence—usually in defense of other inmates." Ntshiza fixes me with this owlish, knowing stare.

I almost feel bad that he thinks so highly of me. "Yes sir."

"As I'm sure you probably don't know, the economy is shit, especially in your hometown area. But Govender—he's your P.O. up north—was able to find you something. It's full-time, night hours. And it doesn't violate your parole, because it's part of the job."

Now I'm more than curious. I lean forward. "What do you mean?"

"You'll be a bouncer at a . . . night club." Ntshiza sort of coughs and clears his throat.

I stroke my goatee, an eyebrow cocked. "A night club, huh?"

He sighs and gives in. "It's a strip club."

"It sounds like you're trying to talk me out of this," I say. There's no way I'd turn this down, even if I wasn't sex deprived. I need a job, plain and simple. I'd take just about anything.

After taking a drag off his cigarette, he flicks ash into the pot of a spider plant. Surprisingly, the thing is thriving, its spindly leaves taking over the desk. He points the cigarette at me. "Don't get any ideas while you're in there."

I lean forward, grabbing my jaw with one hand. "What are you getting at?" I'd never go after any of the women. The only way I'd get into any trouble would be if one of the scumbags there attacked any of the dancers. But like Ntshiza said, it'd be part of the job. There's no way I can fuck this up. I should be thanking him, but I can only stare at him in bewilderment. Not for the first time this week, I'm deeply confused.

Ntshiza closes his eyes for a moment. When he reopens them, he actually looks concerned, as if he's my father trying to teach me something. But those days are long past. I'm old enough to have my own sons. This realization makes me a little sad. So much time has passed, and I've missed out on so much. There's a very real chance that I won't be able to regain any of the things I've lost.

"Son," my P.O. says, "this particular strip club is owned by a motorcycle club. Ever heard of the River Reapers?"

Figures. Pushing my chair back, I stand. "You've had your fun. If you'll excuse me, I need to find a real job." Sooner rather than later. I've only got four weeks left.

"Wait," Ntshiza says. "I just wanted you to have all the details. The River Reapers are in the ninety-nine percent. You have nothing to worry about."

I don't know what any of this means. When I went in, I was just a kid. Now I'm basically just an overgrown version of that same teenage boy. I lean on the back of the chair, draping my arms over it. "Sure," I say, stuffing my exasperation down. "So when do I start?"

"Just go to the club as soon as you get into town. They'll give you your schedule." He slides a folder across his desk to me and crosses his arms.

I guess I'm dismissed.

4

OLIVIA

"Nope. Not doing it," I tell Lucy, crossing my arms.

The motel room is a mess. Crusty man socks litter the floor, his jeans kicked into a corner. Men, I'm learning, are slobs—especially bachelor ex-cons who just got out of prison. You'd think prison would've embedded like a militaristic fastidiousness in him, but it seems like they didn't do such a great job with him.

Not that I have much room to speak. The bathroom counter is seventy-five percent mine, with makeup palettes and hairspray bottles scattered across the fake marble. It's not dirty, though. The counter itself is clean. There isn't even any makeup smeared in the sink—something I can't say for my roommate back in Connecticut.

Still, Lucy insists that I gather all of Cliff's clothing and head to a laundromat. I need to wash a few things, too, but that's beside the point. Family or not, I'm no one's laundress—especially a man nearly two decades older than me.

Lucy and I eyeball each other across the room, her trying to decide how stubborn I'm being and me just, well, being stubborn.

But, I remind myself, our ancestors didn't fight for us to vote *and* do other people's laundry.

"*You* can do his laundry," I say, both eyebrows lifted. "I'm not a maid."

Lucy puts her hands on her hips. She looks more like my mother than my big sister. "Livvie," she says, exasperated. "You need to do laundry anyway. And this way, I can run to the grocery store."

She won't say it, but we're running out of money. We won't be able to stay down here much longer. It doesn't matter how handsome Prince Charming is. Lucy only gets paid monthly, and I'm a student working under the table. If I don't show up, I don't make money. Since I haven't been in Connecticut for the past week, I have zero dollars to my name. Even my cigarette stash is running low—especially with Prince Charming smoking them too.

I'm not trying to be bitter or cranky. Maybe it's having been cooped up in a motel room for almost a week straight, but my mood is pretty sour. There's no doubt about it—I would definitely not survive prison.

Lucy gives me her big sister stare, the one that says "You better not tell Mom or I'll kick your ass." Now that we're adults, it just means "Do this thing or I'll still kick your ass." Sometimes I don't think younger siblings have it very fair. Not even adopted ones.

I throw up my hands. "Fine." Stalking away, I grab my own laundry. "But I'm not picking up all of his dirty socks off the floor."

My mood is pissy. I'm being completely unreasonable. But I can't stop. I'm two minutes away from taking out all of my frustration on Lucy, and none of this is her fault. Maybe I'm even a little bit jealous.

I flop down on the bed. I don't like these ugly, complicated feelings. I just want to have a good time, a couple one-night stands, and finish my degree. It's not too much for a girl to ask.

Lucy sits down next to me, smoothing my hair the way she always has, from the moment I was dropped off at her house as a tiny, scared foster kid. "It's okay, Livvie," she singsongs in a soft, soothing voice.

Guilt pits in my stomach. She shouldn't be comforting me. I'm the one who should be stroking her hair, apologizing for acting like a whiny little kid. Sitting up on my elbows, I shake my head. "No, it's not. I'm sorry." A lopsided smile crosses my face. "I'm just . . ."

"I know." She grins back. "It means a lot to me that you came here with me. It's pretty tough of you."

My shoulders lift and fall. "I guess."

I really don't want to be a burden, the poor little sister who freaks out if she's out of her comfort zone for too long. I want to be adventurous, like the woman I slip on when I go out to bars in New Haven. The woman who flirts with Cliff so easily is only a small part of me. I'm really just ninety-percent rabbit.

Lucy slings an arm around me. "I'll tell you what. Handle those crusty man socks, and I will buy us drinks tonight." She tilts her head to the side. "I *think* Cliff can drink."

A dark bar and Cliff. The thought sends a thrill through me, this weird fluttering in my stomach. "Huh," I say. So that's what butterflies actually feel like. I always thought the saying was just a made-up cliché.

"Deal?" my sister asks.

I don't want to give in too easily. For one, I don't want to be so cheap. Booze can't always win me over. Well, okay, it totally can, but I have to at least appear to put up a fight. Plus I don't want to seem too eager at the prospect of pumping aphrodisiac into the hot guy who has suddenly strolled into my life. Because no matter how often Lucy insists we're family, Cliff is not my cousin. I didn't grow up with him the way she did. He's just another item on my list to tick off.

"Come on, Liv," she pleads. "I'll get us shots and mixers, not just beer on tap."

I'm not playing her. Lucy would've bought Red Headed Sluts

anyway because she hates beer. If anyone is rigging this, it's her. That's how the two-sister dynamic works. Both of us are equally manipulative, in a totally loving, best friends forever way.

I lift my chin. "Tequila shots."

Lucy grimaces. "I don't think I can do those anymore."

"Oh please. You're twenty-eight, not eighty-two. And even then ..." I shake my head at her. "Who else is going to drink with me in the nursing home?"

Groaning, she tilts her head back. "Fine." She falls back onto the bed, eyes bugged out, her tongue poking out of the corner of her mouth.

"You have to do at least two shots before you can keel over," I tell her, prodding her in the ribs with a finger.

She automatically wriggles away, but a tiny giggle also escapes. It's like we're kids again, and she's lunging up from her fake-dead position bellowing "I'm back alive!" It was one of my favorite games, and she's always been happy to oblige me.

This thought makes me feel a *little* guilty, but not guilty enough to budge on the tequila. Someone has to get sloppy drunk with me, and since Uber is our designated driver, it might as well be Lucy.

"Fine." She stands from the bed. "But I'm not at all responsible for my behavior tonight."

Nodding, I stand too. "Good. Neither am I." I toss her a wink, then I follow the trail of shed socks around the room and try to figure out how I'm going to collect them without touching them. I decide that Cliff loses ten hot points for leaving them out, another ten for sweating so much, and ten more for not doing his own laundry. This is actually helpful because he's now hovering at seventy percent hotness, which means I don't want to bang him so badly anymore.

Nothing like domestic bliss to put things into perspective.

"I'm beginning to understand why married people have such

boring sex lives," I remark to Lucy as I pinch a tiny corner of the sock between my fingernails. Depositing it into the dry cleaning bag provided by the motel, I sigh and steel myself for the next one.

"Finally, she comes to the dark side," Lucy mutters.

I glance over. She's sitting at the desk, pen in hand, making a grocery list. We have a mini fridge and a microwave, so my expectations are pretty low. "Is that why you never want to get married?"

There's no answer because the door opens and all six-plus feet of Cliff bursts into the room. His brown eyes are actually smiling, and someone must've taken pity on him because his wild beard has been tamed back into a goatee. He instantly earns back twenty hot points.

"I have good news." His gaze flits from me to Lucy, then back to me.

One of my eyebrows lifts attentively, but I'm so busy wondering why he's telling *me* that I miss whatever good news he wants to share.

"That's awesome!" Lucy flies across the room and flings herself into his arms.

He wraps her in a bear hug, an amused look on his face. "Isn't it? You don't need to go grocery shopping now."

She relaxes into his embrace. "I know," she says dreamily. "We can take the train back and eat at my place."

Clearing my throat, I shake my head. "Uh-uh, we have a deal."

Stepping back from Cliff, Lucy presses her lips together and gives me a little nod. "Yeah, you're right. We need to celebrate!" She hugs him again. "I'm so glad you're coming home," she says into his chest.

A twinge of jealousy runs through me. *I* want to be hugging him, celebrating his good news. It's totally absurd. I don't know him, and I don't plan on it. One night is enough for me, and then it's occasional family gatherings. No hugs or lullabies. I'm going to reintegrate him into society by fucking his brains out, then it's back to class for me.

"And I'm glad I don't have to do laundry now." I toss the bag to the side, then reach for my cigarettes.

"Not so fast," Lucy says. "It's still gotta get done. I'm *not* putting his dirty clothes into my suitcase with my clean clothes."

Cliff glances back and forth between us. He holds up his hands. They're huge and square, perfect for massaging naked breasts. Twenty more hot points, which puts him at 110. Off the fucking charts, even with the crusty socks. Fuck me. I think I'm actually going to swoon.

"You don't have to do that." He smiles at me—really, for real smiles—and nods toward the bag. "Toss that over. I've got it."

Lucy snorts. Both of us turn toward her. "Dude, you don't even know how to do laundry."

He scowls at her. "What do you think I am, a fucking rock? I can figure it out."

My sister's lips press together, and I can practically see the laugh throwing itself at her closed mouth, trying to break through. "What if Livvie goes with you? She's gotta do her own anyway. And mine." She smiles sweetly at me.

"Tequila," I remind her.

She nods. "Have fun."

~

THE LAUNDROMAT IS EMPTY, thank goodness. It's going to be embarrassing enough for the guy to have to be taught how to do laundry. I show him how to load the card at the kiosk, then take him over to the machines.

"You just throw everything in," I explain, reaching for my laundry bag. But I don't take my own advice. Reaching for everything slowly, I pause every time I get to a lacy little thong, making sure he sees it. "Then," I bend over slowly, "you swipe your card, set your time . . ." I straighten and pour detergent and fabric softener into their respective compartments, the liquid a slow drizzle.

When I sneak a glance at him, he's making zero effort to conceal the fact that he's staring at me. Suddenly it really sinks in that we're alone. There's an employee somewhere, probably reading a magazine or watching evening television. Porn-esque thoughts stampede through my head: Cliff shoving me against the machines, his teeth digging into my lower lip as he sucks on it, his knee between my legs.

A whimper escapes my lips.

The heat in his eyes is searing, flames edging toward my skin, threatening to consume me and reduce me to ashes. And I'm not even at all scared. I want it so bad, I'm shaking.

He takes a step toward me.

Swallowing hard, I move in. I've never been one to let anyone else make the first move. I reach for his shoulders, my lips already parting. I'm wetter than I've ever been in my life. This is going to be it, the sex that rockstars write songs about. The kind of sex I can look back on when I'm married with two-point-five kids and I'm covered in baby goo. It'll be the lay to close my list.

I step forward. He closes the distance between us. Rising up on the balls of my feet, I take aim. He reaches behind me. My eyes flutter as I realize he's going to lift me up onto one of the tables and take me right here.

A beep sounds.

I open my eyes. Cliff takes a step back and turns away. The washing machine begins to fill, water and soap sluicing around my clothes.

"Thanks for your help," he says over his shoulder, already setting up his own machine.

Heart thundering in my chest, I make a beeline for the door, a cigarette already between my lips. *Bad girl, bad girl, bad girl*, my heartbeat punctuates my thoughts.

TWO SUITCASES STAND next to the motel room door, our clothing packed and ready to go. The plan is to hit the bar, have a few drinks, then make the overnight train back up to Connecticut. I like this plan a lot, because if I'm drunk enough, I'll actually be able to sleep on the damn thing. Sometimes Lucy truly is brilliant.

She's also a pain in my ass.

"We have to make sure we're like fifteen minutes early before boarding. We *can't* miss this train. I'm leaving the room keys right on the desk, so we're fucked if we miss it. Okay?"

This is the third time she's given us this spiel.

I just nod and continue averting my gaze from Cliff. I'm still so embarrassed. One week, and I'm forever going to be the dirty little cousin in his eyes. It'd be nice if he was completely oblivious about the whole thing, but since he's been avoiding me too, it's not likely.

"Why are you guys so quiet?" Lucy narrows her eyes at us. "I thought we were all excited about this drinking business." She pins me with the super-concerned big sister look.

I want to tell her that was before I made a complete ass of myself, that I'm now thinking I should've waited until we had enough social lubrication to make bad decisions together, but Cliff is already judging me hardcore, and Lucy absolutely can't know. So I just shrug. "I'm tired."

"Good," she says. "That means you won't drink too much."

On the contrary. I'm going to wash this entire day away with Jose Cuervo and enjoy every second of my hangover tomorrow. It'll be like punishment, and it'll take my mind off my still-present lady boner.

There's this patronizing notion that only men need regular sexual affection. Maslow had it right, though—everyone needs sexual healing. And between my last semester, this entire bizarre trip, and now my totally disastrous attempt at seduction in the laundromat, I need some major penile therapy.

Following my sister and Cliff out to the waiting Uber, I pray that there will be one unattached man around my age in the bar who won't mind getting freaky in the bathroom with me. I need to scratch this itch quick, and masturbation ain't gonna do it. Sometimes, a girl just needs some cock.

The Uber drops us off at the least promising looking bar ever. Its facade is small, the bricks grimy. Even the OPEN sign in the window is flickering. Dragging my suitcase behind me, I traipse inside, hoping the interior is better.

It isn't.

The place is so small, there isn't even a pool table. That kills my ol' "Hey handsome stranger, let's play a quick game" routine, and completely eradicates my "Wanna dance?" fallback. Worst of all, there is literally no one here.

A lone woman is tending the bar. She's old enough to be my great-grandmother and looks worse for the wear. This bar wouldn't attract anyone, never mind handsome men in their twenties. I hope she at least makes decent drinks, though I suppose she can't really fuck up tequila shots.

She doesn't even smile as I lean on the bar. Pale eyes stare placidly back at me, zero fucks given whether I tip or not. It's unnerving, but I smile anyway.

"We need six shots of tequila," I tell her, "and open up a tab."

Cliff makes a noise behind me, something between a throat clearing and a growl. It's primal and vibrates through me, even if it is dubious. "I'll just take a beer," he says, voice rumbling.

Why, I wonder, does he have to be so goddamn sexy? Especially if I can't have him.

I peer at him over my shoulder. "Beer? You wait twenty years and you just want a beer?"

Brown eyes challenge me to keep making fun of him. A flicker of that heat from earlier returns. "I want a lot of things," he says in a low voice.

My eyes widen and I grip the bar to remain standing. It occurs to me that he may be fucking with me. I would, if I were him. "I really think you should do shots with me," I whisper back. I bite my lip, wondering what I'm getting myself into. If he's purposely toying with me, there may be a good chance I'm getting my bathroom bounce tonight. But his statement shakes me: *I want a lot of things.* I need to know if he's one of those guys who get very attached very quickly. For all I know, he's been planning his wedding for the last two decades.

"Fuck it," he says, turning to the bartender. "Nine shots of tequila."

She remains standing there staring at us, as if she's booting up. Jesus Christ. I might have to climb back there and serve myself.

Suddenly she jerks away and gets to it. Cliff and I exchange glances, and I wonder if anyone else is here with her. Who the hell leaves an old lady to run a bar by herself? I glance around for Lucy, because she so needs to see this.

At first I don't see her. She's tucked away, sitting at a high table in a corner. Her legs are draped over her suitcase, her thumbs flying over the screen of her phone. Somehow I've got to get her to unwind.

I need to help her get laid when we're back in Connecticut. I know she isn't totally devastated over her breakup, but I worry about her, living in that condo all alone. She doesn't even have a dog.

The sound of a tray sliding over the bar brings my attention back to my mission. I turn to find a tray of nine shots, lime, and salt. Our geriatric bartender winks at me, then shuffles away.

My head whips in Cliff's direction, but he didn't see it. His eyes are burning into me. It's like he already knows how this night is going to end. We're just following a script, playing our roles. My shoulders relax with relief. He won't be one of those clingy guys. This will be so easy.

5

CLIFF

I'm nervous as I carry the tray of shots to the table Lucy's selected. Not because I am prey being hunted, but because I like it. Every time Olivia looks at me with those bedroom eyes, my cock twitches. It's not just that, though.

Something inside me is stirring, like a sleeping beast in its lair. For twenty years I've been dead, but Olivia makes me feel alive. Wide awake and alert, ready for anything.

And I know Lucy won't have it.

She'd be completely right, of course. Olivia is family—my cousin's little sister. Even if she's adopted. Even if we didn't grow up together. I share no memories with her but we share family. Her parents are my aunt and uncle, for fuck's sake. It's one place I can't go—and it's the place I most want to be.

So the shots make me nervous. I haven't had a drink in two decades, never mind motherfucking tequila. There's a reason they call it To Kill Ya. Before I went in, the hardest thing I'd had was a swig of whiskey, and back then I damn near spat it out. Olivia looks at me like I'm this exotic creature, but I'm more like a kid who's just turned twenty-one. I don't know my tolerance level

—and I don't know what's going to stop me from bending her over one of these tables.

I inhale through my nose. Lucy will stop me. As long as she's with us, I can behave. I have to contain myself, because I owe Lucy big time.

We gather around the shots, my cousin eyeing them suspiciously. Olivia passes out the first round. Her tongue darts along the curve of her thumb and finger, her eyes locked on mine.

Christ, I can't even look away.

She shakes salt onto the spot she licked, then hands it to me. I feel like a loser for not already knowing how to do this. Mimicking her, I lick my own hand, which is kind of disgusting. I'd rather lick *her*.

Properly salted up, we raise our glasses in a salute, limes in our other hands. Olivia bellows out a "Bottoms up!" and both women down their shots with ease, lick the salt off their hands, and pop the wedges of lime into their mouths. They watch me with matching green smiles.

"Fuck it," I mutter, and copy them.

The tequila is the worst thing I've ever tasted, but I've long mastered a stone face. I slam my empty glass down and start passing the next round.

"I guess you aren't such an alien after all," Lucy remarks as she salts her hand.

I cock a "Nope" eyebrow at her and raise my glass.

Olivia bumps my arm gently with hers and clinks her shot glass against mine. "To freedom," she says. Her eyes never leave mine as she takes the shot. That velvet tongue caresses her hand, salt shining in the dingy light as it dances in her mouth. Then she sucks the lime into her mouth real slow, her lips pulsing around it.

I need some distance between us, stat.

I rush through my shot, chasing it with one of the remaining three on the tray. I wipe the salt off on my jeans and ditch the lime. Then I'm across the bar and out the door. It doesn't take long. The bar is small.

The icy winter air is even better than a cold shower. I walk a little away from the bar's facade, gulping in arctic air. Leaning against the bricks of another building, I tip my head back and close my eyes. The alcohol pumps through my system, a dreamy dizziness carrying me off. One shot was probably enough.

A silky voice warms me up. "Smoke?"

My eyes open. Olivia stands in front of me, a cigarette extended. One is already lit between her lips. I swallow hard and take the proffered cigarette. Before I can ask for a light, a flame flares from her hand in front of me. She holds the lighter steady until I'm lit, then pockets it.

"Now you owe me seven years of good sex," she says with a wink. Her words aren't even slurred. We're not playing on fair ground. Her brows furrow. "Or I owe you. I forget which it is. Either way." Those eyes smolder into mine. She steps forward.

I'm still leaning against the wall, so there isn't really anywhere to go. I stop her with an arm, holding her in place. "We can't," I rasp while exhaling smoke into the night.

Her head tilts. "Can't talk while smoking?" Either I'm drunk or the corners of her mouth really are curled upward.

"I know what you're doing." The world is blurry around me. Not the way it looks, but the way it *feels*. Everything is fuzzy. Beer buzzes have got nothing on tequila drunk.

"What am I doing?" She sucks on the cigarette several seconds longer than necessary. "I'm just smoking." Her eyes drop to the hard-on in my jeans. "What are *you* doing?"

"Christ." I shake my head. "I'm not doing this."

Olivia takes another step toward me. "Why not?"

Because a thousand reasons. They all fly through my head and into the night. I rub at my chin with my free hand. "Fuck," I rumble. I can't think. I don't know whether it's her or the alcohol, but...

I freeze.

"You did this shit on purpose," I say through a sandpaper laugh. "You got me drunk and now you're trying to cart me off somewhere."

"Well," she says with a straight face, "there wasn't a pool table."

I blink at her in confusion. While I'm trying to figure it out, she stands up on the balls of her feet and grabs the back of my neck. Instantly I lose control.

I spin her around, dropping my cigarette and pressing her against the wall. My knee parts her knees, my arms caging her in. For a second I breathe in the scent of her hair. It smells dark, sweet, and euphoric. The feelings pounding through me have nothing to do with the alcohol I've consumed.

It's all her.

I lean down, soaking in the scent of her skin: clean and feminine. My nose brushes her cheek and my lips hone in.

My mouth brushes hers. Even in my inebriated state, I want to enjoy every second of this. Because it will never, ever happen again. I drag my lips against hers, and she shivers. She's immobile in my arms, not because I'm crushing her but because she's just as earnest to enjoy the moment. We both know this is the only one we'll ever get.

But she's hungry, and her lips part. Teeth sink into my lower lip, and her mouth closes around me, sucking and licking. My cock twitches again, every pint of blood in my veins hurtling into it. This is a complete waste.

It's been twenty years.

I'll be lucky if I last five minutes.

"Fuck." I pivot away from her, trembling with control thrashing at its cage, begging to be loosed. I stalk away several paces, my hands clenched at my sides. I don't want to be the worst she's ever had. I want to be the man who makes her realize she's never truly had sex. Not until me.

This is no good at all. I really am a teenager all over again.

Her arms wrap around me, fingers plucking at the button of my jeans. "I don't care," she whispers into my back. "I want whatever you've got."

This woman can read minds. I should be terrified, but I'm just turned on even more. It's as if she knows me, like she's always been lurking in the shadows.

Like we've just been training for this moment.

It's a mindless, drunk thought, but it erases any shred of guilt I have remaining. I turn around and wrap my arms around her. "Lucy," I remind her, speaking into the top of her head.

She rests her forehead against my chest. "Yeah," she sighs. "I guess we'll just have to be honest."

Releasing her, I stumble back. "Are you fucking serious? Do you really think she'd go for this?"

Olivia shrugs. "Who cares? I thought you just meant she's in there all by herself." Her eyes dance with the unspoken dare.

"I'd rather she not find out." I shove my hands into my pockets. This woman drives fucking holeshots around me. And I don't even care. It's been a week and I'm already addicted. I wonder if this happens to every man who does time. Do we just imprint on the first woman we come across on the other side? What I'm feeling for her probably isn't even real. It's just desperation, the primal urge to sink into something I haven't had in a long time.

I'm only a man, but even still, I don't want to use her like that. This woman deserves fine dinners and coffee in the morning. I'm not saying I want to put a ring on it, but it feels wrong to fuck her and duck out.

Maybe I have done my penance after all.

"Look," Olivia says, dragging me out of my thoughts. "Luce has never interfered with my love life. Or sex life." She grins mischievously. "She may not approve, but she doesn't get to tell me what to do. Or you, for that matter. Just because she came down here and bought you clothes—"

I hold up a hand. "Don't say that. This is flat out disrespectful, and you know it. We're . . ." Family, but I can't even say the word. This is all so fucking wrong.

She hisses a laugh. "We're *not* family, if that's what you were going to say. You're a man, and I'm a woman. We're two people with the same itch, the lock and key. We need each other." Her eyes grow two sizes and her voice drops. "I need *you.*"

I'm too drunk. I can't dodge her shrapnel. And she's right: we're both consenting adults, and we're not related by blood. No one is committing a crime. It's better to just get it over with while we're still drunk. Then we can go back to what we were doing before.

We've been outside "smoking" for so long, I'm surprised Lucy hasn't come looking for us. Sucking in a deep breath, I drop my shoulders, all the fight melting out of me. Not that I was putting up much of a defense. All I can do is hope that this isn't one colossal fucking mistake.

"You're out of cigarettes," I say. "Let's go get some more."

Her eyes drop to her pocket. "No I'm not." She fumbles out her pack. "Look, still got like ten." She lights two at once and passes me one. "Now eight."

I take the cigarette and walk down the street, away from the bar. She'll figure it out and follow me. And if she doesn't, I'll just have to deal with this raging erection myself the old fashioned way. No harm, no foul. I'll leave it all up to her.

Footsteps behind me tell me that fate has taken my side. Olivia catches up and tucks her hand into mine. We walk and smoke in silence, my eyes scanning the area around us, looking for a place. There's no convenient alley, no restaurants with bathrooms. It's mostly a residential area.

After what feels like an hour, I stop walking and turn toward Olivia. I shake my head. "This isn't going to work." The tequila is still floating in my veins, dragging me into the undertow. I drop my arms and pin Olivia with a concluding gaze. Maybe fate wasn't on my side after all.

"Hold on," she says, glancing up and down the street. There's a dangerous look in her eyes, one that simultaneously draws me in and makes me pause. This woman might look harmless, but she's a criminal when it comes to sex. She grabs my hand and tugs me forward, trying car doors as we walk.

She's dead serious.

"Olivia, what the fuck are you doing?" I mutter. "I'm on parole. You know that, right?"

She tosses me a challenging look. "Is your probation officer here right now?"

"No, but—"

"Relax," she says, pulling the door of a station wagon open. "We're not technically breaking in if it isn't locked."

There are so many technicalities wrapped up in this night.

She climbs into the back seat, shedding clothing. "It's roomy in here," she purrs, beckoning me inside.

With one more glance at the street, I climb in after her, shutting the door behind me.

Our breath steams up the windows. She peels off garments, flinging them onto the passenger seat. Within seconds, she's naked.

"Your turn."

So much for savoring this.

I yank off my jeans, shirt, and coat. My cock stands at full attention. Olivia regards me with an amused expression on her face. Heat flushes my cheeks. "What?"

"You were commando?" she asks, crawling into my lap.

I laugh. "I ran out before, and didn't get a chance to change after we did laundry."

Olivia smiles back. A wisp of hair falls into her eyes. I brush it back gently, my eyes roving over her face. Suddenly we're shy teenagers who thought they were ready but don't really know what to do next.

My hands drop to her hips, fingers caressing the soft flesh. "You really want this?"

She nods. Her arms encircle my neck, those eyes locked on mine. It could be a trick of the light, but she looks truly happy. Maybe she's one of those people who really, really like sex. Whatever the reason, I'm honored to be the one to make her feel good —in multiple ways.

Soft lips tug at mine, her tongue flitting across my bottom lip. She sucks me between her teeth while her hands trail to my shoulders. The heat radiating from her warm center is so inviting.

My tongue plunges into her mouth, a growl escaping my lips. I should be gentle with her, but I don't want to. I want to consume her until I'm completely intoxicated, neither of us able to walk.

Her legs wrap around my waist, her hips thrusting her soft wetness against me. Fingers from one hand pluck at my nipples, while her other hand wraps around me.

In just a few seconds, I'm going to throw back the bars of the cage. "One more time," I growl into her mouth. "Do you really want this?"

She rubs the head of me against her slit in response.

Her slick wetness makes me come completely undone. In one motion, I twist our bodies until she's flat on her back. Her legs wrap around me, and I lower myself until I'm throbbing at her entrance. Olivia gives me a final nod, and I slide in.

Her warmth envelopes me, and I almost come halfway through my first thrust. "I'm not going to last long," I choke out.

"Shh," she soothes into my ear. "It's okay. Just give me all you've got, baby." Her arms lock around my neck and she clings to me with her whole body. I sheath myself in her, embedded deep inside.

Slowly, I slide out, until just the tip of me is in her. I caress the side of her breast and each rib with my fingers as I make my way down to her. I want this to be just as good for her as it is for me.

Stroking her with my fingers, I plunge into her again with slow precision. With each thrust, I get more into a rhythm, two knuckles grinding against her. She shivers underneath me, tiny moans tumbling from her lips. Hard nipples rub against my chest, a complete parallel to her soft breasts pressed to my pecs. Our hearts pound against each other, blood boiling, edging us closer and closer.

My cock surges, the fire of the orgasm blowing through me.

"Fuck," I growl into her ear. "No."

She gasps, shouting out. "Just fuck me," she pants, and I do. I plow into her, rubbing her, begging her. This will all be for nothing if I can't take her with me.

Olivia arches into me, her back coming straight off the floor. A moan ripples through the station wagon, her nails raking down my back. "Yes, baby, yes," she breathes as she shivers against me.

The last twenty years rush out of me, pulsing into her. I feel her tighten and expand around me, driving us both into the abyss.

It's the best I've ever had.

I collapse, rolling to the side so I don't crush her. A stream of hot liquid gushes down my thigh. Resting on my back, I stare at the ceiling, my breath ragged. Beside me, she exhales and turns onto her side.

"Wow," she says, grinning. "Thank you." She dips her chin. Our eyes meet for a second, then she reaches into the front seat for her cigarettes. The flash of bare skin exposes a twin stream running down her leg.

My heart just about stops.

"Fuck," I say, scrambling to sit up. "We need to get to a store. We didn't—I mean, *I* didn't—"

She glances over her shoulder. Now she really does look

amused. "Relax," she says, handing me a cigarette. "I'm on the pill."

I fall back, relief rushing through me. I smoke in silence, and decide I've had enough thrills in one night to last me a lifetime. From here on out, I'm keeping my head down and playing it straight.

This can never, ever happen again.

6

OLIVIA

I want to shout to the world that I just had the most mindblowing sex in the back of a broken-into station wagon. Every inch of me tingles, my entire body vibrating with electric current. But Cliff and I just walk back to the bar, smoking cigarettes without speaking. It seems like we're both on the same page, because he doesn't mumble any lies about going out to dinner or anything. By the time we get back, the tequila is wearing off and I need another drink to celebrate.

Bursting inside, I wave to Lucy and march up to the bar. Our elderly friend is still back there, drying off clean glasses. It's got to be like midnight, so it's unbelievable that she's somehow still awake.

Since I've already had four tequila shots, I think it's best to just continue with my friend Jose. "Tequila Sunrise, please," I say, leaning on the counter.

Someone pinches my arm.

Lucy stands next to me, glaring. "Where the fuck have you been?" she hisses in a low, dangerous voice.

I lift an eyebrow at her. "Getting cigarettes. What's the problem?"

"The problem," she says, waving her phone in the air, "is that we missed our train."

I start to argue with her, to tell her that what she's saying is ridiculous. Then the phone slows enough that I can read the time. My mouth falls open.

"Yeah." She crosses her arms. "So you wanna try again?"

Cliff slides onto a bar stool on the other side of Lucy. "What's going on?"

My sister spins around on him so fast, *I* see stars. "I told you two that we couldn't miss this train! There isn't another one 'til the morning. Do you *want* to spend the night sleeping at the train station?"

He rubs at his face. "Aw, Luce, I'm so sorry. I think the tequila disagreed with me. I needed some air, and then Olivia said she was going to the gas station. I walked with her, but I got sick on the way. She was trying to protect my manhood."

I nearly choke on my drink. Sugary sweet liquid trickles down my shirt. Putting the drink down, I dab it up with a cocktail napkin before Lucy sees.

My sister deflates. Somehow, she has this super soft spot for Cliff. He could tell her the world is flat and she'd believe him. I'm even more curious than ever now.

Lucy hops up onto a bar stool, then gives Cliff a one-armed hug. "Lightweight," she says. She orders a soda, and Cliff throws me a wink when she's not looking.

I exhale and try to enjoy my drink. The danger has passed. Lucy won't find out, and Cliff and I will go our separate ways. It's the best possible outcome for a one-night stand—my absolute favorite ending to a beautiful fairytale.

I lift my glass toward him in a salute, and drain it.

THE NEXT TRAIN to New Haven isn't until seven in the morning.

We close out the bar, granny still wide awake. Then we take an Uber to the Harrisburg train station. Since it's an hour long ride, I rest my head against the window of the back seat and try to fall asleep. Cliff sits between us, with Lucy on his other side. It's how we've been taking Ubers late at night. I know Lucy won't sleep, because she doesn't trust anyone. But I trust Cliff. We finally have a bond, and since we've swapped DNA, we might as well be family.

A giggle bursts from my nostrils. I glance at the others, but none of them even notice that I'm still drunk. Snuggling up into the most comfortable position possible, I close my eyes and say goodbye to Lewisburg. It's been real.

When I wake up, we're just pulling into the parking lot. I still really think Lucy would've saved money had we just driven down here, but instead of pointing that out, I touch ground and stretch my stiff legs. Cliff jumps out behind me, his hands tucked into the pockets of his coat.

"We still smoking buddies?" he asks in a low voice.

"Of course." I hand him my pack and lighter. This time he lights two and hands me one. "What a gentleman." I wink.

He winks back.

I smoke, trying to slow my thundering heart. I'm too tired to start analyzing what that wink means or why I'm still reacting so strongly to him. My body should be satisfied, still swimming in sweet memories. It may have been short, but that was still the best orgasm I've ever had. Peeking at him out of the corner of an eye, I wonder whether I'd ever really done it right before. Maybe it's because he was an exceptionally attentive lover. Most of them aren't.

All these thoughts just make me want to find another car to break into. Shaking them off, I toss the rest of my cigarette and follow Lucy inside. It's time to enforce that no-clinging rule for myself.

During our overnight stay in the train station lobby, I make sure I look at him as little as possible. I don't stop sharing my cigarettes, because that's cruel and unusual in the smoking circle, but I do stop talking to him. Even though we sit next to each other on the train with Lucy across the aisle, I keep to myself. I ignore the heat radiating from him and those smoldering eyes, burying our night where it belongs.

In the past.

THE NEXT DAY is for recovery. Lucy drops me off at my apartment, and I don't waste any time with sappy goodbyes. I'll talk to Lucy in a couple days or so, and I'll see Cliff at the next family reunion. Easing inside, I pull my luggage behind me, then close the door quickly. A tiny meow alerts me to Dio's position. The orange tabby kitten comes hurtling at me, the bell on his collar jingling. I let go of my suitcase and scoop him up, nuzzling him against my face.

"Hi buddy," I croon. "I missed you."

He wriggles in my hand and meows again sternly.

"I know, baby. I'm sorry I left you." Carrying him with me, I head into the kitchenette. It isn't far. Our place may be laid out like an apartment, but I've seen bigger motel rooms. Dio's probably still too little for kitty treats, so I've been spoiling him with something I think he likes even more.

I open the refrigerator and retrieve the container of grated cheese. Tapping out a teeny bit into my hand, I carry Dio to the counter. Then I put him down and he makes a beeline toward my fingers. His sandpaper tongue brushes against my skin as he laps up every last round white crumb. Before my roommate can see him on the counter, I place him back down on the floor.

He's the only male I'll ever commit to.

"Our little secret, right bud?" I leave him in the kitchen and go to put my things away. Esther is apparently at class, so once I'm unpacked, I snuggle up with Dio in my bed and turn on a Netflix movie that I promptly fall asleep to.

Even though I take such a late nap, I go to bed pretty early, too. When I wake up in the morning, I feel refreshed for the first time in the past week. Booze, good sex, and a full night of sleep will do that for a girl. I hang out 'til it's time to dress for work, give Dio one last chin scratch, then get going.

Most of the undergrad students I know at Southern have jobs on campus, or relatively close. Not me. I stopped living on campus last year when I found an even better job right in the city I grew up in.

I catch the bus and take it downtown, then walk down a couple streets. Though it's in a questionable area, I've never felt unsafe. I carry a knife and mace in my bag, and I've always been great at screaming "Fire!" Anyone who tries to hurt me will be very, very sorry. I'd rather die fighting than do nothing.

A squat, wide man at the door gives me a nod. I smile back in greeting, then continue my trek to the back. The place is empty at this hour, but some of the girls are hanging out and practicing. I say hi to a few on my way to Mark's office.

Pausing in front of his half open door, I smooth my hair. Mark is that boss who always hits on everyone. He's harmless so I never dwell on it. Besides, I'm not his type. He prefers blondes. Still, I want to be extra sweet to him because he was pretty cool about me taking off for a week. He's always been good to me.

I push the door open, but my knees turn into water.

A man with a broad set of shoulders stands with his back to me. I'd recognize that physique anywhere. After all, two nights ago I was skin to skin with him in the back of a station wagon on a dark street. I'm intimately familiar with the muscles of that back, their hardness beneath my fingers.

I stand frozen and speechless until Mark notices me in the doorway.

"Hey kiddo," he says, gesturing me inside. He turns to Cliff. "This is Olivia, one of my girls. Olivia, Cliff is our new bouncer."

Cliff turns slowly in my direction. Those thick lips part, his eyes widening. I think of them locked on mine as he drove in and out of me. I feel myself clench, hot and wet, as I remember how hard and thick he was. The breath in my lungs whooshes out.

Bouncer.

You've got to be fucking kidding me.

I look back and forth from Mark to Cliff, trying to decide whether this is all some big joke. Maybe they know each other from high school or something, and thought this would be funny. But neither of them look amused. Mark is completely oblivious, because he's a man in his mid-forties. Cliff looks like someone just kicked him in the nuts.

Recovering, I hold out my hand. "Bouncer, huh? It's nice to meet you."

His hand grasps mine. Brown eyes funnel into mine, holding me, mesmerizing. "Dancer, huh?" His words are strangled.

I have to press my lips together to keep from laughing. Our hands remain clasped, and I squeeze his fingers. "That wouldn't break our agreement, would it?" I keep my eyes wide and run my tongue along my lower lip.

Cliff swallows, but doesn't drop my gaze. "It definitely makes things a little harder," he says with a straight face.

Coughing, I release his hand. I turn, reaching for a tissue from Mark's desk. I pretend to blow my nose, then straighten. It'd serve him right if I keep messing with him, but he's going to find out within the next half hour, anyway. "Come on, I'll show you my work station."

His expression is unreadable, but there's a flicker of something in his eyes. Kinda like a mix between fear and desire, like he can't wait to see me on the pole and then take me in my dressing room, but feels guilty about it.

I lead him to the bar.

"Cold water?" I ask, tossing him a bottle. I lean on the counter and watch as he twists it open and gulps half the thing down in one shot. Beads of sweat stand out at his hairline.

He shakes his head. "You enjoy this way too much."

"But you make it so easy." I chuckle and grab myself a bottle of water. In the past week, I've made him turn a certain shade of pale at least three times. Not always on purpose, though. I couldn't have planned this one if I'd tried. And it definitely throws a wrench in my love 'em and leave 'em routine.

Cliff sits down and runs a hand through his hair. "Jesus Christ, Olivia." He shakes his head again. "You couldn't have given me a heads up?"

"Why?" My eyebrows scrunch together. "How the hell was I supposed to know you got a job here?"

He scrubs at his face with his hands. "Luce didn't say you work at a fucking strip club."

"That's because *Luce* doesn't know." I cross my arms and narrow my eyes at him.

Making a frustrated sound, he downs the rest of his water. He leans forward. "What else are we keeping from her?"

"We won't tell her about the baby, either." I watch him, unblinking, as my words sink in.

But he chucks the empty bottle at me. It bounces off my shoulder. "Be serious, Olivia." He points a finger at me. "This isn't going to work."

I hiss out an exasperated breath through my teeth. "So, what, you think I'm just gonna walk away from my job? Fuck that, and fuck you." I don't remind him that I was here first, because this isn't high school. But I *am* concerned. Usually my nighters are guys I'm positive I'll never run into again, or only occasionally. No one from classes, for example, but upperclassmen I run into in the student center are fair game.

Groaning, Cliff places both hands flat on the bar. "Here's how this is gonna go, then." He stands up and leans toward me, towering over me. "You stay in your corner, I'll stay in mine. Lucy doesn't find out. We don't talk." He pats the pocket of his coat. The outline of a pack of cigarettes shows through. "Cool?" His eyes are nearly black.

"Sure," I tell him. I turn away, busying myself with getting things ready for the night. It's a ladies' wristband special evening, so I make sure all the bottom shelf liquors are in the right place. Some of the girls who work here know jack shit about booze hierarchy. When I turn around a minute later, he's already gone. I frown. I don't like how I'm feeling.

Like I've been written off.

It's unfair, considering I didn't want anything more to do with him. But I hate how easily he can set the rules all the same. Maybe it's because usually they're *my* rules. Which is pretty ridiculous, considering we're on the same page. I should be celebrating, but instead my eyes dart back to Mark's office, where Cliff is bullshitting with him. Both of them laugh, and Mark glances my way.

"What the fuck?" I mutter. I'm about to stalk over there when music blares over the sound system, Theory of a Deadman's "Bad Girlfriend." Scowling, I shoot a look at the girl on the stage. It's a terrible song, and dancing to it is a complete cliche. It doesn't matter what I think, though, because this place brings in a lot of money. The customers tip well, even if they're all bikers with hungry eyes.

The Wet Mermaid belongs to the River Reapers and serves as their club house. I suppose that makes me a house mouse, even though I don't usually sleep with any of them. Every once in a while a nomad or someone from another chapter will stay for a bit, and we'll have a little fun before he leaves. But I've never been a back warmer and I'm relatively unassociated.

I just work here.

The frown continues to crease the skin between my eyebrows. I can't believe any P.O. would hook an ex-con up with a job in a known MC club house. The River Reapers aren't really outlaws, but it's still like pairing up Chuckie the killer doll with Chuckie Finster from Rugrats. I still don't know what crime Cliff committed. The MC sells baby drugs like weed and pills, which is much more profitable than bouncing and all too tempting for someone who's been in the system.

At least, I'd think so. But I'm just a peon working on her undergrad, studying social work—not a P.O. Still, it bugs me.

Biting my lip, I decide I have to go to Lucy. Cliff just can't get involved with these guys, not if he wants a fresh start.

7

CLIFF

Besides my great big surprise, The Wet Mermaid is exactly as I expected. Mark runs me through my responsibilities for the night. It's so straightforward, anyone could do it, but I guess they need someone who looks imposing. Mark introduces the guy I'm shadowing tonight as Beer Can, then leaves us to it.

Beer Can looks me up and down, arms crossed around his round torso. Gray streaks his black hair and beard. Despite his short stature, the dude is solid. He could be a Viking warrior. "You looking to patch in?"

Most of the guys here wear leather jackets or vests with the River Reapers insignia: a sludge reaper with water snakes wrapped around it. It's a nod to the nationally known pollution level of the Naugatuck River due to illegal chemical plant dumping. Supposedly the river is actually clean now. Back in elementary school, kids whispered stories of two-headed fish and more sinister creatures.

I give Beer Can a shrug. I'm here for a job. At least, I thought I was. It's really fucking weird that my P.O. would hook me up with this place.

Beer Can leans in. The patch on his breast reads SGT. AT ARMS. "Between you and me, kid, you're better off. On the outside, you need family." He claps my shoulder twice. "Hang around, get to know everyone. You might like it."

I glance away. I might be green, but I've been around long enough to know that it's pretty rare for MCs to invite in outsiders —especially nobodies like me. Either someone is fucking with me, or these guys are desperate. Whatever it is, I want no part of it.

Beer Can leans against the door frame. "Now, most of this gig is carding kids. Don't know what it is, but they always think they're gonna pull one over us." He spears me with dark eyes, face even darker despite his fair complexion. "Everyone gets IDed, even old men with oxygen tanks and walkers, got it?"

I nod. Out of the corner of my eye, I catch a flash of bare flesh. One of the girls swings around the pole, legs a blur. Working here is going to be a pain in the balls.

"While we're on the list of *dos* and *don't*s, our girls are off limits. No palming asses or stealing kisses. They're all club property. We clear?" Beer Can may be all of 5'6", but he's no one to piss off. If push came to shove, it would be a close fight.

"You don't have to worry about me," I say, thinking of Olivia.

"Good." Beer Can jerks a thumb toward the bar. "Every once in a while, fights'll break out. Usually it's just brothers messing around. Maybe someone had too much to drink. Sometimes it's about a woman. We don't run into too much trouble. Mostly it's about flexing muscle, separating 'em. You know, kids in opposite corners." He strokes his beard. "Though sometimes we just let 'em at it, if it's a good match."

I think of all the fights I've seen in the past two decades. "I once saw a guy get his head kicked in."

"Not here." Beer Can laughs.

"So no rival clubs storming in?" I keep my voice light and conversational, but I am curious. Mostly because I don't want to get mixed up in that shit. Plus there's Olivia to think of. I think I have to tell Lucy, which is going to be a problem because then I might have to mention the other night. But I can't let Olivia work here. I don't know what the fuck she was thinking, but even if the River Reapers aren't outlaws, they're still dangerous.

Then again, so am I.

Beer Can shakes his head. "None of that shit." He claps my shoulder again. "We have fun. We ride, throw parties, sell a little coke."

Christ. "Thought it was just Percs and shit?" I cock my head at Beer Can, who gives me a smug shrug. With every passing second, I'm more and more anxious to get Olivia out of here. She's a college girl, for fuck's sake. There have to be a hundred jobs at her school, yet she picks a drug warehouse fronting as a strip club.

This job is going to be temporary for both of us. There's no way my P.O. did this knowing what's going on here. Normally, I wouldn't care, but I'll die before I go back into that concrete tomb.

"Relax, kid," Beer Can says. "If I were you, I'd float on this parade while it lasts."

Before I can ask him what the fuck that means, a tall, broad-shouldered man wearing colors strides up to us. He glares down at me with hazel eyes, even though we're about the same height. The patch on his breast reads PRESIDENT.

The President holds out his hand. "I'm Ravage. Good to finally meet you." As we clasp, his gaze holds mine. Respect flickers in them. It takes me by surprise.

I glance from Ravage to Beer Can. Maybe it's my time still haunting me, but this whole thing has me uneasy. I don't know what to expect or what they expect from me. And even though I'm sure they're great guys, I can't believe any rational P.O. would send an ex-con to join a biker gang.

"I'm sure you've got questions for me," Ravage says. "Then

there are a few guys who would really love to meet you." He jerks his head, indicating for me to follow him.

Beer Can gives me a nod and returns to his position at the door.

I follow Ravage into a sort of conference room. A huge tapestry embroidered with the club's insignia takes up a whole wall. Various photos and items with club colors decorate the rest of the walls. Ravage sits at the head of the heavy oak table and motions for me to sit too. "Is Mark gonna be cool with this?" I ask.

Ravage smiles. "Mark is our Treasurer. He answers to me." He jabs a thumb at his chest. "Don't worry about him." Leaning back in his seat, he swivels a little to the left, then a little to the right, back and forth. Just watching me.

Waiting.

My brows furrow. I want a simple life. No games. A job to come home from. Eventually a place of my own. I think of Lucy's spare bedroom. Good thing she decorates in neutrals. Then, as if by default, I think of Olivia.

Ravage nods at me, that smile still there. He oozes understanding and respect. It's fucking weird. "I get it, man. Fresh out— everything is surreal. But I made a promise, and I'm gonna hold up my end of the bargain. I always do." He places both hands on the table, palms down. "Fire away, kid."

I start with the obvious. "Why did my probation officer connect me with this job?"

Ravage shoots me a superior look. "Because no one else around here will hire a convicted felon." He leans forward. "But we do. We have an arrangement with local law: send us your convicts, and we won't cause any trouble. Mostly." His smile is feline and predatory. "We also get a nice tax break, so I owe you another thank you."

"Another?" I'm scowling so hard, my face is going to get stuck this way. I don't believe any of his bullshit. Whatever his game is, he's playing me.

"Relax," he says. "We didn't bring you here to cause trouble." He drums thick fingers on the wood. His voice drops conspiratorially. "Everyone in this town knew what was happening to that poor little girl. It still boils my fucking blood." Face clouding over, he looks away for a moment. "We don't tolerate that shit."

My face relaxes an iota. "Why are we talking about Lucy?"

Ravage straightens. His eyes meet mine, awed. "You did what none of us were able to do, son. When you went in, we took a vote. I promised to watch out for you when you got out."

I should ask him where the fuck they all were a week ago, but I don't. Mostly because I still don't understand the game. Thoughts are knocking around in my head like a bunch of bumper cars. I need a cigarette, some time to sit down and make sense of this. Because it's completely upside down.

"We can't have shit like that in this town," Ravage continues. "It's wrong."

He says this with such conviction, it surprises me. Everything I know about bikers is compounded into one rule: stay away.

"We were fractured," he continues. "Couldn't come to an agreement. Any decision had to be unanimous. This club was split into two, and there was nothing I could do about it. And then you came along." Despite the light from the overhead lamp, Ravage's eyes are hooded, shadows painting his face into an angel of death. "Killing him wasn't against club rules, because you weren't a member. You did us all a favor, kid, so now it's time for us to repay you."

The room spins as he stands. His words replay in my head, my brain trying to catch up. I must've been one naive kid to have missed something this big.

Ravage slides a leather vest across the table to me. My eyes snap up to his. I start to shake my head.

"It's a brand new world when you realize who your father really is," he says quietly. "But you're a better man than he was."

I trace the insignia that is embroidered into the leather with a trembling hand. Surreal doesn't even begin to cover what's happening right now. "I don't even have a bike," I tell Ravage, voice hoarse. I need a drink. Or a whole bottle. Even though I wasn't actually manipulated, I feel used. But that's not all.

"We have plenty," the President says. Like it's that simple. They can just give me a bike and I'm ordained.

As I trace the sewn on Prospect rocker, an entirely new feeling envelopes me. It brings me back to my childhood, when one-year-old Lucy giggled for me for the first time. We were at my parents', and she'd asked for a cookie. My mother told her no, that it was too close to dinner. As soon as she left the room, though, I climbed up onto a chair and grabbed one of the soft chocolate chip cookies from its packaging. Breaking it in half, I handed one to Lucy. She tapped hers against mine and giggled, an announcement of camaraderie.

I haven't felt anything like it in twenty years.

My eyes meet Ravage's. He gives me a nod.

"Go ahead, son. Try it on."

So I do.

The cut-off vest has a weight to it that isn't just the leather. It's brotherhood, but it's also a major responsibility. It's the unasked question that is heavy on my tongue. I'm afraid to voice it, because I already know the answer, and I don't like it. It means that there's no escaping who I am, that the very thing I hate is embedded deep in my veins. The only way to get rid of it is to spill every drop—but I don't believe in that.

My choice is obvious: either I embrace what I am, straddle the point of no return and ride it out, or I walk away. The answer comes easy because there's nowhere else to go. I'm not leaving Naugatuck and Lucy. There's also Olivia to think about, but I can't get started on that just yet. I've got enough to chew on.

Ravage sends me off, telling me he'll knock my teeth out if I go back to the door—Beer Can's got it. I'm supposed to wander around, meet my future brothers, and enjoy the party. Turns out they're closing the place to River Reapers only.

We're celebrating me.

What I did.

I walk straight to the bar. Olivia is chatting with a woman whose bronze skin is so deep, it's actually black. The other woman would normally be my type: long curly hair, round eyes, supple breasts that I can grab onto and hold. If Beer Can hadn't told me to keep away from the girls here, she'd be my new class crush. Maybe the rules change when you're fully patched.

Olivia eyes me as if she knows exactly what I'm thinking. She gives her head a tiny shake and shifts her eyes toward a purple-haired Puerto Rican woman at the other end of the bar.

I see the glances they exchange, and it's obvious: they're together.

Fair enough. It's not like I can stop thinking about Olivia, anyway. Working here is going to make it even harder to stick to our arrangement.

The curly-haired woman carries two fresh drinks over to her girlfriend. They look at each other as if they're the only two people in the world. I want that. I really do. But there isn't a single woman in this world who would want that with me. She'd have to be irrational, and I don't fuck with unstable chicks.

Olivia examines my vest. "That was fast."

I slump onto a stool. "I need a drink. Anything."

She frowns, but pours me a Jack and Coke. "Want to talk about it?"

Sipping my drink, I consider the idea. Confiding in her would be typical boyfriend/girlfriend behavior, though—strictly against our agreement. So many rules bind me now. And here I thought I'd gotten out of prison.

"Don't worry," she says. "Bartenders are like therapists without the pay. You talk, and I'll keep the drinks coming." She winks and lights a cigarette.

For the first time, I notice that everyone is smoking freely. I light one too. "We won't get fined for this?"

Laughing, Olivia raises her cigarette in a salute. "All the time. Naugy makes a lot of money off us. We all chip in to cover it."

I lean on the bar and drop my voice. "Do you have any idea what's going on here?"

She shrugs. "Why would I? I'm just the bartender." She takes a drag, then exhales into the smoky air. "Most guys would kill to wear that, you know."

"They sell drugs, Olivia. This is just a front." And fuck knows what else they do. I don't say that, though. "This isn't a good place for you."

The relaxed woman in front of me morphs before my eyes. Her eyelids droop so that only slits of her pupils, irises, and whites are showing. Her lip curls. Nostrils flaring, she stabs the cigarette into the air in front of me. "You don't get to tell me what to do."

"Look, I'm not trying to be a dick, Livvie—"

"And you *don't* get to call me that." She sucks in a long drag. "The only way this is going to work, Cliff, is if you do you and I do me. We agreed: family reunions. That means you don't stomp around acting like my fucking daddy."

I rub my temples. "So you don't mind working in a place that sells coke?"

The dirty look she tosses me is simultaneously condescending. "What the fuck do you think I do behind this bar? Pour beer for shit tips?"

Oh, Olivia. I look down at my drink, at the cigarette in my hands. I need something a lot stronger. It's only my first shift and everything is spiraling out of what little equilibrium I had. "You'll go down with them," I say. "Do you want that?"

She rolls her eyes. "I *want* to pay off my student loans. The most I can possibly hope to make is $40,000 a year in this fucking state. I'll be lucky if I can land a job with DCF. I don't want to start off in debt right out of the gate."

"What is it you're going for?" I pictured her as doing something more adventurous, not sitting in a goddamn state office all day.

Stubbing out her cigarette, she settles those brown eyes on mine. "I want to be a social worker. I wanna help kids in the system." The unsaid remainder of that sentence hangs between us: *So they don't end up like you.*

"Don't you think," I say slowly, "that it'll be a little hard to get a nice state job if you're convicted of selling drugs?"

"Fuck you," she lobs at me.

Grinning, I stand. "You already did." I walk away, the whiskey soaking into me. Not in an out of control way. My veins swim, limbs relaxed. This head is clear.

The overhead speakers crackle, and the music switches from modern shit I've never heard to nineties grunge and metal. Soundgarden's "Black Hole Sun" spins, the two girls on the pole whirling with it. I watch them for ten or so seconds before I move on.

This is my party. I might as well enjoy it.

Brothers pass me beer and clasp hands with me as I make my way through. Every one of them is welcoming, some of the older ones even thanking me. I guess the younger members wouldn't really know about what went down.

I'm not even sure I do, anymore.

They make the eighteen-year-old Cliff who saved Lucy sound like a hero. But it wasn't like that. Not for me. It feels wrong to celebrate it. I may have protected Lucy, but the price I paid is acid eating at my soul. The man who walked out of penitentiary is not that teenager. From one second to the next, I'd transformed into something unrecognizable. A dark, insatiable creature.

Most people would be horrified if they had to do what I did. No matter how hard I try to feel otherwise, I enjoyed it.

I revel in every moment that replays in my head.

The only part that I would take back is Lucy, huddled in the corner, screaming with horrified eyes locked on me. As if I was the monster instead. Even still, there's no doubt in me that I would do it again.

A man with red hair and a beard streaked through with a few grays claps me on the back. I read VICE PRESIDENT embroidered on his chest. "Welcome home, Cliff." His light eyes are sincere, shimmering with joy.

If someone had told me someday I'd bring a whole club of bikers happiness, I would've laughed at them. I'm not laughing now.

Turns out whiskey chased with lots of beer is so much safer than tequila. "Thanks," I reply. My shot nerves are swimming in alcoholic bliss. Apparently I'm at least ten times more sociable when I'm drunk. I make a mental note not to get too fucked up that I can't talk to Lucy when I get home. She needs to know about Olivia.

"Everyone calls me Skid," the Vice President says. "It's a long story."

Beer Can slings an arm around each of us—my waist and Skid's shoulders. "It's actually pretty simple. Skid here dumped his bike but wasn't wearing anything else." He grabs Skid's arm and rolls up the black sleeves he's wearing under his cut, exposing a rash of pocked, whitened flesh. It's at least ten years' healed, but still angry.

Both men laugh.

"You should see the rest of me," Skid tells me.

"Don't worry," Beer Can assures me. "I'm teaching you how to ride tomorrow, not this asshole."

Billy Idol pumps over the speakers, and my mood lifts even more. Even if I'm wary of joining the MC, I have to admit—at least to myself—that I'm drawn to it. The notion of cruising down Naugy back roads with so much power between my legs and a whole family of brothers around me is such a good one, I can almost overlook the drugs. Give me a week and I'll probably be completely ambivalent about it. Knowing what I know now, this was inevitable.

I've finally come home.

Beer Can waves several dollar bills and staggers toward the stage, leaving me and Skid in the middle of the club.

The Vice President leans in, eyes glinting. "I got you a little something, kid." He jerks his head for me to follow him. I stumble in his wake, suddenly more drunk than I thought I was. It's still just a nice buzz, not anything I'm going to wake up hungover with. I follow Skid to a door that takes us into a hall. We pass customer restrooms and the dancers' dressing rooms, then come to a flight of stairs.

It occurs to me that he might be taking me up to the roof so he can shove me off. No one knows where I am. Olivia is busy at the bar, probably pissed off at me, and Lucy is at home doing lesson prep for her students tomorrow. My fists flex. If he's looking to punish me for what I've done, he's going to get a hell of a surprise. I'm just as brawny in a fight as I'm built.

But we emerge onto a second floor. Skid gestures to the partially opened doors lining the halls. "By now you know The Wet Mermaid is also our club house. We keep rooms up here for some of the guys. Not you—you're still a Prospect. But for tonight, we all kicked in and got you a little something."

He pushes the first door open.

A brunette with deep olive skin is spread across a made full-sized bed. Her breasts rise and fall with each breath. My eyes trace the swell of them, the way they slope into her belly. I follow the invisible trail to her parted legs. One arm is slung across her belly, her delicate fingers slipping low. "Hey papi," she purrs.

"Door number one," Skid says. He nods down the hall, takes a couple of paces, and opens the next door. This one houses a red-haired white woman, equally bare except for the fiery patch of hair between her legs. "Door number two." Skid grins. "And so on and so forth."

I laugh. "I think you're overestimating my libido."

Nodding once, Skid grips my shoulder. "That's why you've got to build it back up." With his free hand, he gestures to a door. "Your choice. Enjoy." He claps me on the bicep and wanders away.

"Christ," I mutter. My brand new biker family has bought me a game show's worth of prostitutes.

I pick a door at random. It feels offensive to choose based on the women's looks.

The woman behind my door has long, wavy brown hair. Her nipples peek through the strands. "Hi honey," she says, stroking the creamy skin of a thigh. "Come on and join me."

Her eyes aren't as luminous, but she still looks too much like Olivia. The animal in my pants relaxes as my heart clenches. Fuck me, but Olivia is the only woman I want.

But she doesn't want me.

Even then, I can't just forget about her. It's as impossible as changing my DNA. For better or worse, she's a part of who I am now.

"Sorry," I tell the woman. I turn around, and close the door.

8

OLIVIA

The weekend passes in a blur of work. With each shift, I'm more and more annoyed with Cliff. Still, I've got to tell Lucy—as soon as I get out of class. Monday came way too quickly.

"Morning," my roommate Esther yawns as she pads into the kitchen. Dio darts around her feet, nearly tripping her. "Ay dios mio." The tiny cat pauses and looks up at her, his head cocked to the side.

Laughing, I finish spreading cream cheese on my bagel. "You have to admit, he's really cute."

Esther holds up a finger. "I admit nothing." She continues her trek to the coffee pot.

I wink at Dio. Give her a few more weeks, and she'll be snuggling with him on the couch. I carry my bagel and coffee to our little table. It'll be a half hour or so before Esther is even ready to go. She stumbles toward the table and joins me, her own mug clutched in both hands.

We caffeinate in silence. It's not that Esther is standoffish. She's just an introvert. If she's not at work or class, she's in her room or on the couch, reading a book. Maybe binge-watching Netflix.

"Olivia," she says suddenly.

My head snaps up. "Yeah?"

"I just wanted to let you know," Esther says, frowning into her mug. Her dark eyes meet mine. "Some guy came by looking for you last night."

I roll my eyes. Fucking Cliff. My fingers curl into fists. This is the last time I ever have a one-night stand with someone I know I'm going to see again. Gritting my teeth, I shake my head. I can't believe he's doing this shit. Whenever I next see him, I'm putting his ass in line. Better yet, I'm going to text his ass. I glance around the kitchen for my phone.

"See, I thought he was acting kinda weird." Esther touches my hand. "Should we call the police?"

"No," I grumble. "He's my . . ." I bite my lip, trying to decide how to describe him to her. Definitely not "cousin."

"Boyfriend?" Esther guesses.

"*No*," I say a little too forcefully. "It's complicated." Great. Now I feel like a Facebook status.

I get up and hunt for my phone, leaving Esther to finish her breakfast. She's my ride to campus, so I can't exactly get pushy. Instead I've learned to get up and ready early, that way I can read for class or sneak in some Netflix while I wait for her. Our arrangement has been working for the past four years. I'm not sure what's going to happen when we graduate. Esther's grandparents pay for her apartment so she can stay close to home. They have all three of her younger siblings, though, and I think it's kind of understood that once she finishes her undergrad, she has to take the kids. I don't know the details, because she won't talk about it and I'm not one to press.

It might sound selfish, but I'm really not looking forward to having to find my own place. Then again, I can probably crash at Lucy's in the meantime—as long as Cliff is out of there.

I snatch my phone from within the folds of my comforter on my bed and fire off a text to him. "You can't just show up at my place. It's not okay." Placing it on my dresser, I wander my room, grabbing the textbooks that I need. It's wild that this is it—my last semester.

I've thought of going on to get my Master's, but I'm itching to get into the field. I've never exactly been patient. Which is why tricks like getting up early and staying occupied have kept me from falling apart every time Esther runs late. I've learned to give her an earlier time than necessary. Works like a charm.

By the time my bag is packed—including extra snacks—Esther is ready to go. She's a whirlwind of hair tucked into a messy bun, leggings and UGGs, and a half-zipped backpack. We walk out to her car together, the bright winter sun piercing my vision.

It's a surprisingly warm day for February. Spring is in the air, and it puts a bounce in my step. Things in my life are really coming together.

The ride to Southern is always quick—until we hit New Haven. Esther eases into traffic and turns up the volume on KISS 95.7. "If we're going to inch along, we might as well have good music."

I nod in response. The latest Beyonce song really isn't my thing, but my roommate adores her. It's yet another contrast between us, one more reason why we're more acquaintances than friends. But Esther is nice, and sometimes she'll cook for us. Usually I order takeout for our dinner. She's the closest thing to a friend that I've got—besides Lucy.

The thought of Lucy reminds me that I need to tell her about Cliff. I'm not really sure how I can rat him out without giving myself away. I sigh.

"What's the matter?" Esther asks. Route 63 dumps us out onto Whalley Avenue. She takes a left onto Blake Street, speeding into the turn before the green arrow goes out.

My lips part to tell her at least a little about Cliff. I can't. It's bad enough that he's legally my cousin. Throw in the part about him being on parole, and it just all looks awful. I shake my head. "I just can't figure out why the fuck he'd show up at our place," I murmur.

"Maybe to win you back," she says. "Did you fight?" She rolls to a stop at the intersection.

I glance at the gas station on the corner and realize I'm out of cigarettes. Esther will never go for it, though. I may be on time, but she's running late. "Something like that," I tell her with another sigh.

Cliff has me doing all kinds of things I don't normally—like thinking about him and sighing like a school girl. My nose scrunches. Fuck Cliff. I need to get back in the game, keep moving. I can't let him get to me like this.

Esther hurtles onto campus and drops me off in front of my building. "I'll text you when I'm on my way," she says, and peels off.

Shaking my head at her, I glance around for a victim. There are always smokers around, and there's usually someone willing to let you bum one. I've handed out more cigarettes than I can count. Karma has to kick in at some point.

I spot a familiar looking figure. His back is to me, his lean shoulders hunched against the wind. It's always windy at Southern. I approach him, fur-lined black leather boots sloshing through half-melted snow. He cups a cigarette with one hand, a lighter in his other hand. The wind keeps knocking out the flame.

"Here," I say, holding my hands out.

He glances at me and smiles. "Oh, hey." He hands me the cigarette and lighter.

Using the wall as a partial block, I light the thing in one shot. The single drag I take instantly soothes my nerves. I pass it back to him.

"Nah." He plucks out another from his pack. "You earned it."

As we smoke, I peer at him. "You look familiar. Do we have class together?"

Sandy hair hangs in his eyes. He shakes the strands out of his face and nods. "Photography."

Right. I had two elective slots, so I picked some things that I thought might be fun. Only I hadn't counted on needing to buy a camera and a bunch of other stuff. I'd thought the school would provide them. "That's later this morning, isn't it?"

"Eleven-ish." His green eyes search mine expectantly. "You don't remember my name, do you?" He chuckles.

"Sometimes I can barely remember my own," I say, holding out my hand. "Olivia."

His hand takes mine, his grip warm. I notice a cross tattooed on his index finger. "Eli." His gaze holds mine, hungry. Between that longish hair, those greenish brown eyes, and the tats, he just might be one-night stand material. He's only in one of my classes —a class I'll probably drop anyway.

"Are you Italian, Eli?" I drop my voice and hold his gaze. I need to get Cliff out of my system, and Eli is perfect. He's just desperate enough that he'll be easy. Southern is a big place and I don't even live in New Haven, so even if he gets any odd dating ideas in his head, it'll be simple to avoid him.

"Why?" he asks, his voice husky. "Do you like Italian food?"

I picture him in my mouth and nearly choke on my cigarette. "Only if I can eat it off of you," I purr. His eyebrows lift, lips dropping open. Men are so easy—every single one of them. All I have to do is flirt with them a little, and they're putty in my hands. I bet this one would eagerly follow me into an empty classroom right now, like a hungry puppy. I take another drag while I consider putting his leash on. I can probably ditch my child welfare class. I'm ahead of the reading and even before I left, it was a pretty easy course. I've always been a good student.

"Ah, shit. I'm late. I'll see you later," Eli says. He lifts a hand in parting and jogs away.

I was too slow.

It's probably just as well. I don't want to earn a reputation around campus. Besides, my little meatball is probably Catholic and looking to settle down with fifteen kids the second he gradu-ates. With my luck, I'd get knocked up the one time and would have to at least humor the idea for a little while.

Besides, Italian food isn't really my thing.

Still, I could really use the distraction. I walk to class chewing on the inside of my cheek, wishing I could get Cliff out of my head. This has never happened before. It's ridiculous and it needs to stop. Yes, he's sexy and he makes me laugh, but I can't let myself get carried away. If I sleep with him more than once, I'll end up dating him or something.

Maybe Lucy isn't the only one with a warped sense of romance.

I stride into class promising myself two things: I'm going to tell Lucy about the club, and then I'm never going to think about Cliff again.

ESTHER IS SUCH A DOLL, she drops me off in front of Lucy's. The street is dark and quiet, the temperature back at a proper winter freeze. I wave to Esther as she pulls away, then let myself in.

I find Lucy in the kitchen, several notebooks and her planner sprawled about the table. "Lesson planning?" I ask, pulling up a chair. I pour myself some coffee from the carafe into the extra mug she's left out. Lucy pretty much assumes I'm coming over at this point.

"Ugh," she replies, rubbing her temples. "I just can't figure out how to teach these kids this Common Core math shit. They're in first grade, for fuck's sake. It shouldn't be this complicated for them."

I grimace in agreement. I've seen some of the things she

teaches, and it makes my non-math brain hurt. "Take a break." I reach for her hand and gently pull the pen from her fingers.

She groans but complies. "What's up with you?" she asks me over the rim of her coffee mug.

Shrugging, I give her my most innocent smile. "I think I might've found my next guy." I wiggle my eyebrows.

Lucy nods for me to continue. "Don't leave me hanging. I live vicariously through you, remember?"

"Well," I say, leaning forward, "there's this hot guy in my photography class."

She holds up a hand, palm out. "Whoa, whoa, wait. *You're* taking photography?"

I clear my throat. "C'mon, Luce. Leave that shit in the past, where it belongs." I try to sound flippant. My cheeks redden in rebellion.

"You're never gonna live that one down, Livvie." Laughing, she tucks strands of hair behind each ear. "I can't believe they're trusting *you* with a camera."

"I was nine," I remind her, "and I have to buy my own. I was wondering if Dad would let me borrow one."

Lucy snorts. "Are you high, kid? Dad's memory still works just fine."

"Hmn." I tuck my chin into my hand. "I guess you're right." Glancing around the room, I try to figure out how to broach the subject.

Lucy suddenly grabs my hand, her eyes intent on mine. "Listen, Livvie, I want you to know . . . I know. And it's going to be okay."

Freezing, I blink back at her. "Do what now?"

Cliff steps into the kitchen, whistling Bush's "Glycerine." His taste in '90s music is approval-stamp worthy. He strolls to the refrigerator and peers inside. "Do we have any leftovers, Luce?" he asks, completely ignoring my presence.

I set my mug down hard. "What do you mean, you *know*?" I ask Lucy. My glare is still fixed on Cliff's back, though.

"About the strip club." My sister's eyes mist with worry, her eyebrows turned down. "I know you want to pay your loans off, hon, but it's not worth selling your body."

I swear, Cliff's shoulders shake with laughter.

"I'm *not* stripping," I tell her. "I'm bartending. The tips are good, especially if you show a little cleavage." I point at Cliff. "*He* just joined the fucking River Reapers." Even though I'm trying really hard not to, I sound like a little kid. Then again, the fucker tattled on me first.

Cliff's shoulders stiffen.

"They sell drugs out of that bar," I tell Lucy. "I know because I pass them to customers with their drinks." It's too late to clap my hand over my mouth.

Cliff joins us at the table and pours himself coffee. "Well, isn't this nice," he says, glancing from Lucy to me. "All our cards are on the table. Except yours, Luce. Any illegal activity you want to share with us?"

Lucy sighs, rubbing her temples. "What the hell is wrong with the two of you?" We both open our mouths, but Lucy shakes her head. "I don't want to know about what you're doing. I've got enough to do. Keep your dirty little secrets to yourselves." She pulls a notebook toward her and bows her head.

My whole face is on fire. Cliff is pointedly not looking at me. Shoving my chair back, I stand and motion for him to follow me. I stalk outside and light a cigarette, marching back and forth along the front walk. I stomp up to him. "What the hell is the matter with you?"

He lights his own cigarette, inhaling. Seconds drip by as he unleashes a stream of smoke into the cold air. He grins down at me. "I'm just looking out for my *cousin*."

I start to jab the cigarette into the air in front of him, to tell him off. I really, really want to kick him in the ankles.

He shakes his head, still smiling. "Want to go for a ride?" He nods to a motorcycle parked in front of Lucy's. I should have noticed it when I came in, but I was too preoccupied.

"Asshole." I give his arm a playful shove, but the hard muscle underneath his long-sleeved shirt and leather vest is totally distracting. My eyes trace the way the vest hugs his muscular torso. "You wear that thing well," I say with a sigh. At least I can say I tried to get him out of there. Too bad Lucy is too busy with work. Then again, I'm lucky she didn't press me to make sure I'm not really stripping.

Cliff nods. "Thanks." It's hard to read his face in the dark, but he sounds weird. Kind of hoarse.

"Late night?" I ask, taking another drag.

"Nah." Looking back at the bike, he shrugs. "Just a long morning." His eyes snap to mine. "So what's with you and the photography guy?"

I laugh. "You were listening the whole time?" Taking a step closer to him, the corners of my lips lift in a coy smile. "Naughty boy."

"I can show you naughty," he says, and my heart combusts. "So," he draws out the word as his eyes hook mine, "how about that ride?"

9

CLIFF

Even though I'm taking it easy, wind whips my face as I cruise down 63, Olivia tucked against my back. Beer Can's motorcycle lessons might've been rigorous, but it's already second nature to me. Or maybe it's just my blood, the tide finally coming in and reclaiming the shore.

Still, I'm not great with turns just yet, so I plan to just take her straight down and then back. I ease into a gas station, teeth gritted. If I dump us, I'll never forgive myself. We make it in one piece, though, even if my turn was too wide. Beer Can promised I'll get the hang of it, that I'll be flying up and down the back roads with the rest of the club in no time. If I don't, I guess they'll realize their mistake and turn me out.

Balancing the Screamin' Eagle between my legs, I shut the engine off. It continues to vibrate through me, my blood singing. This whole thing should be unnerving, but I'm thrilled. Every step into the club just draws me in deeper. But I've promised myself I'm not going to be like *him*. I'm already better.

Instead of climbing down, Olivia remains snuggled against my back. "That was nice," she murmurs.

She's so warm. The wisps of her spirit wrap around me,

claiming me. This woman is going to completely undo me if I can't have her. I want this moment to last, but she'll think something's up if I linger. I have to let it be exactly what it is: a ride. Nothing more, nothing less.

Untangling myself from her arms, I swing off. "Need anything?" I ask, nodding to the gas station.

She shakes her head dreamily. "I'm coming in with you, though. It's cold."

We walk inside together, my head still trying to catch up with my actual life. A big part of me is still inside, lying on my bunk staring at the ceiling between shifts. Not only has a motorcycle club taken me in, but they've also given me a beast of my own to ride. The Screamin' Eagle is almost a decade old and club property, but it fits me like a glove. And the most beautiful woman I've ever seen is riding home with me.

Well, not *home* home.

The gas station attendant perks up when he sees my girl. He's cut but wiry. "Hi Olivia." His eyes practically laser into her, ignoring me. I instantly don't like him. His gaze is too intense, his eyes too vacant.

"Oh, hey Eli." She smiles. "I didn't know you live out here." Leaning on the counter, she looks too damn familiar with him.

My fists clench inside their leather gloves.

"I just work here," Eli says. "It's still close enough to campus."

My eyes hood in suspicion. If I remember correctly, Olivia's school is in New Haven. It's about thirty minutes from Naugy. And I *don't* like the way he's looking at her. "I need a pack of Marlboro Blacks."

Eli sets his jaw, his sandy douchebag haircut flopping. "Yeah, in a minute," he says, as if I'm a fly he's trying to shoo out of the store.

I bow my head, eyes locked on his. Deliberately, I nuzzle my nose into Olivia's hair, inhaling her scent. That dark jasmine envelopes me, damn near making me dizzy. I pull her closer into me. "Time's up."

Olivia cocks an eyebrow at me over her shoulder. "Cliff," she says, almost amused, "this is Eli, from my photography class."

The hot guy. Of course.

My lip curls into a sneer but my arms remain locked around her. If she wants this asshole, there's nothing I can do about it— but right now, she's out with *me*. "How nice," I say. My stare never leaves his face. "Marlb Blacks. Now."

He snuffles a laugh, eyes flicking from me to Olivia. "He your friend?"

"I'm not going to ask again." The words are careful, measured. Dangerous. Blood pumps through me, and the familiar anticipatory thrill of a fight awakens me. I outweigh this guy by at least fifty pounds.

Olivia sighs and tips her head back, exposing her creamy, pale throat. I want to sink my teeth into her, to hear her gasp and scream as she comes. She rolls her eyes at me. "You can take the convict out of prison . . ." she intones, a smile tugging at the corners of her mouth. It's even more thrilling, knowing that she's amused. I could beat the guy to death and she'd still be laughing. At least, that's how it feels.

Photography douche's eyes snap to attention. "Prison, huh?" He smirks, crossing his arms. "Is it true what they say?"

Behind that jerk facade, though, he's practically sweating bullets. "What?" I ask, my voice low. My fingers brush Olivia's hips. "That we're feral when we get out?"

Olivia peers over her shoulder, eyebrows lifted, lips parted. Her wide eyes are luminous and shimmering with lust as she arches into me.

It's my turn to smirk.

Eli tosses a pack of cigarettes at me, his entire face sagging. Something clicks in his eyes over and over, like gears in a broken windup toy. I reach for my wallet, but he holds up a hand. "They're on me." Cold eyes tunnel into me.

I slap money down on the counter anyway, then wrap an arm around Olivia's waist and lead her outside.

Olivia glances at the gas station over and over as I start the bike. I'm not a one kick wonder yet, so it always takes me time to get the thing going. Which is really useless in a time like this when I'd love to rip right out of here.

The Screamin' Eagle roars to life. Olivia hugs me as we take off back into town. Since the passenger seat is several inches higher than mine, her lips easily brush my ear.

"What was that all about?" she asks over the engine.

My shoulders stiffen. "I don't like that guy," I call back.

I don't hear her sigh so much as feel it. "He's letting me borrow one of his cameras," she says.

"There's something wrong with him."

I turn onto Meadow, the short street that's one of many hills that populate Naugy, my teeth clenched. It's steep, and going down was a lot easier. Riding this thing takes so much concentration. There's a lot of respect and trust involved. It's me and this machine, working in tandem.

As we near Lucy's, Olivia wraps her arms even tighter around me. "Are you jealous?" she purrs into my ear.

There's a hell of a lot of implication behind her words. It gives me a headache, trying to figure out where she's heading—whether she's angry or pleased. She is so much goddamn work.

I say nothing as we roll quietly onto Lucy's street. I park the motorcycle, but neither of us move. The night presses onto us, winter's last few ounces of strength. Soon the weather will be good and I won't have to worry about killing myself on icy streets. Tonight the pavement was dry but tomorrow it'll be back to bumming rides from Lucy. Despite what Beer Can says, I'm not comfortable enough to ice skate. Yet.

"You are," Olivia says softly.

"What?" I shift in her embrace and look at her over my shoulder.

Solemn brown orbs measure me. "Jealous." Her lips curve around the word.

I hold her gaze and drop my voice. "Maybe."

Her grip on me tightens. "Take me home." The heat smoldering in those words blasts into me.

"Olivia." Her name is a soft whisper of agony, a warning. "You don't want to get involved with me."

She huffs daintily. "Who said I wanted to date you?" Her eyes glint. "I just want to fuck you."

My head shakes. "I can't do that." Nodding toward Lucy's, I don't vocalize my thoughts. I shouldn't need to.

"But you can tattle on me," Olivia says. She pulls away, the sudden loss of her warmth leaving my back cold.

I groan inwardly and light a cigarette. "I thought you only liked one-night stands."

"Maybe I want to make an exception."

Drawing in a breath, I start to remind her of Lucy, but she holds up a hand.

"She's already told us she doesn't care." Hugging herself, she stares at me, leaving the ball in my court.

"And Eli?" The name is bitter on my tongue. I've known her for less than two weeks, and I'm already seething at the idea of her with another man.

The look she shoots at me says enough, but she gives it to me anyway. "So let me get this straight," she hisses, keeping her voice down so we don't rouse the neighbors or my cousin. "You don't want me?"

"I didn't say that," I sigh. I hand her my cigarette. "I'm just saying . . ." Christ, I don't even know what I'm saying. I should be warning her off. There's something stretching inside of me, eager to be let out. And even though it should scare me, it doesn't. I'm not reckless enough to do anything that will land me back in

Lewisburg, but I've been given my freedom and the opportunity to use it to its fullest potential. I don't want Olivia involved in that. It's bad enough she works at The Wet Mermaid.

She watches me expectantly, waiting for me to finish.

"I'm dangerous, Olivia." I throw the words at her.

Rolling her eyes, she takes a drag off the cigarette. "You're such a fucking cliché, *Cliff*." She shakes her head in contempt. "I'm not on my knees begging to marry you and have your babies. I'm inviting you to my apartment for sex between two consenting adults who are mature enough not to make it personal. My roommate is working and I'm horny." She puts her hands on her hips. "You can't bend me over a counter and then leave me hanging."

She looks so fierce, a smile cracks my lips. "Well, when you put it that way, Ms. Reynolds . . ."

Stomping her foot, she tosses the cigarette into the street. "Just take me home and fuck me."

"Get on the fucking bike, then," I growl back. This woman is giving me whiplash, and I'm not sure I can take it. As she climbs back on behind me, the cold hard truth sinks in.

I like her—*like* her, like her.

As pathetic as this might sound, I've never had a real girlfriend. I mean, I've had girls. I wasn't a monk in high school. From the time when I was fifteen to right before I got locked up, I always had someone. None of it was ever serious, though. We didn't do things like go to the movies or hang around the mall like you see on the Hollywood big screen. Maybe in another life I would've taken those girls out. I don't know. My parents weren't even married, so dating wasn't exactly a priority.

The thought of them points me down a path I don't want to walk, so I lean into the wind and focus on getting to Olivia's.

She guides me to an apartment complex on the edge of town. I get us as close to her door as I can, then kill the engine. Dismounting, I turn to face her. She straddles the pussy pad, watching me. I don't wait for her to get off and go unlock her front door. Lifting her into my arms, I sweep her off the bike, cradled to my chest.

But as usual, Olivia has other ideas.

She wriggles in my arms until her legs are wrapped around my waist, her arms slung about my neck. "What are you gonna do to me?" she asks.

I blink down at her, my brow creasing slightly. "Isn't it obvious?"

Rolling her eyes, she grinds her pelvis against me. "I mean to punish me. For making you jealous."

"This is all just a fucking game to you, isn't it?" I carry her to the front door, pinning her there while she fumbles in her bag for her keys.

"Well, yeah." Tender pink lips part as she laughs at me. She places the keys in the palm of my hand, and I close my fingers around them.

I press into her until my lips are a whisper from hers, her body trapped between mine and the door. "If anyone's being punished," I rumble, "it's me." My lips capture hers, pressing flesh hard enough to bruise. I wanted to go slow, but the way she's talking to me loosens all of my knots. Through the rough denim of my jeans, I ache for her. I grind against her, those legs tightening around me.

She gasps into my mouth, and I know neither of us are into taking our time.

I jam the key into the lock, twist the knob, and shove the door open. Carrying Olivia inside, I slam the door shut with the heel of my boot. The layout of her place is open. I walk us down a short entryway, past a tiny kitchen and into the living area. Two doors oppose each other. "Which room?" I rasp between fevered kisses. She points and I follow.

This time, there's no need to rush. We're not stealing time in the back of a station wagon. I grin as I move us into her bedroom. The room is dark, heavy black curtains keeping out the light from the street. Her mouth works down from my lips, trailing wet heat and nips down my throat. Moaning, I dump us both onto the bed.

I yank her jacket off, tossing it to the floor. Her shirt follows it closely, my hands curling around her firm, supple breasts. I catch a nipple between my teeth, my tongue flicking at it. In response, she arches against me, crying out. The second she recovers, her fingers work at my jeans, peeling them off.

I wrench off her leggings. The sound of ripping fabric cuts through the air. I stop, panting above her on my knees. "Sorry." I'm being too rough. Tipping my head back, I suck in a deep breath, trying to collect myself. I'm four times her size. I have to be careful with her.

But Olivia collides into me, her lips and teeth yanking at mine. "Don't worry about it," she breathes during a moment when our tongues aren't interlocked. "They were from Forever 21. Can't really expect much."

She finishes removing my clothing, then curls her fingers around my length. Giving me a hard tug, she pulls me toward her and lies on her back. "Round two, baby," she says.

Even if the leggings were just thin fabric, she isn't. I enter her slowly, savoring every inch that I gain into her pulsing wet warmth. She rocks against me.

"Yes, baby, yes," she whispers breathlessly.

All of the most powerful substances in the world have nothing on the potent high she gives me.

I slide fully home, and for a moment we just look at each other. Her breasts knead my chest, her nipples still hard. Our hearts beat in tandem, and the notion of how in sync we are makes me fucking dizzy.

She lifts an eyebrow at me. "You gonna stare at me all night, or are you going to fuck me?"

Letting out a hoarse laugh, I slide out until just the tip of me is touching her. "Just remember, you asked for it," I tell her, hesitating just one more second.

"Yes, I did," she says in the most angelic voice.

I glide back into her in one quick thrust, eyes locked on hers, making sure she's okay. She rolls her eyes at me and bucks right back up at me, her pace matching mine.

I give it to her, everything I've got, everything I've been holding back and dreaming of these last twenty years. Our bodies disconnect and reconnect with lightning speed, Olivia clinging to my back, thighs shuddering and mouth crying out in pleasure with every blow. It's the kind of sex that feels so good in the moment and leaves muscles pleasantly sore the entire next day. The concept is familiar, but with Olivia it's like nothing I've ever experienced.

She rakes nails down my back, teeth grazing my shoulder. She begs for it harder, even as I'm sweating, muscles trembling, the cords in them standing out as I work to keep up. My black hair hangs in her face and she takes fistfuls of it, pulling so hard I swear it's going to come straight out of my head.

Yet every second of it drives me closer and closer to the edge.

I can feel it building, that liquid fire that sparks somewhere in my belly and shoots through me.

"Come on, come for me, baby," she coaxes into my ear.

"What about you?" Each word is forced, all of my energy focused into not ejaculating.

She laughs softly. "I already have, like seven times." Fingernails dig into the tender flesh of my ass, forcing me even deeper into her. "Let it go, baby."

She's the one pulling the strings, because she doesn't get halfway through her sentence before it rips through me. My head tips back, my entire body jerking. Even in the throes of my own climax, I can feel her seizing around me.

We come together and collapse into a heap on her bed. I pull her into me, wrapping my arms around her, and press a kiss to her shoulder. If what I feel so far is infatuation, I'm a little afraid to see what it'll be like to love her.

I'm addicted.

She shifts in my arms, breaking free. Standing up, she begins collecting clothing from the floor. *My* clothing.

"Not a cuddler, huh?" I smirk. It's just as well. I need a cigarette. Sitting up, I stretch.

She tosses my clothes at me. "My roommate will be home any minute. Time for you to leave."

Olivia pads out of the bedroom. A few seconds later, the shower faucet squeaks and water pounds the tub. The bathroom door shuts with a loud thump.

Holding my jeans in my hands, I wait for her to shout for me to join her in the shower, to tell me she was kidding. Several minutes fly by. Ducking my head, I close my eyes. I've been duped.

Thankfully, Olivia won't ever know that I stood naked in her bedroom, waiting like a hopeful puppy. I tug on my jeans, shaking my head at myself. Dio meows from a corner, the closest thing to a cat laugh that I've ever seen.

"Yes, I know," I tell him softly. "Can you blame me, though?"

He closes his eyes and buries his face in his paws.

Even though I'm not sure I deserve to, I wish things were different—that Olivia and I could eventually have the type of relationship where I stay the night. I'll take what I can get, though.

Shrugging into my cut, I leave Olivia's place, my skin already cold without her touch.

10

OLIVIA

I can't help but sing while getting ready for class the next morning. Part of me feels like an asshole for kicking Cliff out, but Esther really was coming home, and I didn't want to deal with her questions. Neither of us have ever brought a guy home before—usually I go to their places. I've also never slept with the same guy twice.

Cliff has me breaking all kinds of rules.

I throw on sweats and my high top Nikes, then toss my hair into a frizzy bun. With such wild curly hair, I'll never have one of those cute messy buns that straight-haired girls rock. But I've managed to make it my own.

I'm supposed to work tonight, but I'll come home and shower first. Still, just in case, I wing my eyeliner and dab on mascara. Looking at my reflection, I shake my head at myself. The odds of me running into Cliff today are pretty low. This is totally absurd. After another moment, I shrug and add lip gloss.

My hand is on my bedroom door knob when I hear a door slam. Frenzied shrieks and Spanish gush from my roommate's mouth. I throw my door open and Esther barrels into my room.

Between high school and my roommate, my Spanish is pretty

good, but she's talking way too fast. Tears streak her cheeks, and she clutches her phone in her hand. I lead her to my bed and sit her down. After bringing her an ice cold glass of water, I calm her enough to talk.

"My car," she gasps, her hands shaking. "Someone slit my tires."

I bolt up straight. Eyes narrowing, I stomp toward the front door as if I can still catch the motherfucker. Right outside our front door, Esther's car slumps pathetically. All four tires have long gashes in them. My jaw hangs open even as fury rips through me. Esther is a nice person—someone so quiet, she wouldn't disturb a librarian. Cutting tires is never random, always personal. This doesn't make sense.

I light a cigarette and Esther joins me outside. Red rims her eyes and blots her nose.

"Who would do this?" she whispers, hugging herself.

I shake my head. "No one followed you home?"

"Not that I saw." She holds her hand out for my cigarette. I give it to her and light another for myself. Taking a drag, she grimaces. "I haven't smoked since high school." Still, she visibly relaxes. Once a smoker, always a smoker.

"Anyone you might have . . . annoyed?" I can't imagine Esther ever pissing anyone off enough to make them want to slit her tires, but I have to cover all the bases.

Her head swivels from side to side. "No. Last night was actually a really good tips night." Dainty eyebrows knit together. "Donny even asked me out."

My eyes narrow. "Who's Donny?"

Lips softening into a smile, Esther practically swoons. "This guy at work. He's one of the chefs. I've been waiting for him to make a move forever." She sucks on the cigarette, still smiling.

"He's nice to you?" I'm losing hope. Walking around the car, I examine it again.

"Very," Esther says. "He's one of the ones who hold doors open

and all that. He's even brought me gifts—little things like chocolate. He brought me a rose last night."

I blink at her.

Rolling her eyes, she puts her hands on her hips. "Valentine's
Day?"

I halt in my tracks, groaning. "Fuck," I mutter.

Esther rushes to my side. "Did you think of something?"

"No." I sigh, lighting another cigarette. "I kind of did something last night, without realizing what day it was." Wrinkling my
nose, I hope Cliff didn't think it was all supposed to be some
romantic bullshit. Or, even worse, that I was so desperate for a
Valentine, I begged him to come home with me. I rub my
temples. God, I'm pathetic.

"Jesus," Esther says in a strange, breathy voice.

My eyes snap to her, then follow her gaze. Carved into the
trunk of the car are the words HAPPY VALENTINE'S DAY
CUNT. Rushing to her side, I wrap an arm around her and guide
her to the curb.

I guess Donny isn't so nice after all.

As soon as I finish smoking, I run inside for an extra can of
mace. I explain to Esther how to deploy it during the Uber ride to
school, and also give her an extra knife. "He's probably pissed off
that you didn't bang him in the supply closet or something," I tell
her. "So you might not ever need this stuff." Part of me wonders
whether we should have called the police and filed a report, but
it's useless. Naugy cops are assholes, and they'll probably only say
something racist to Esther, like "I'm surprised you speak
English."

Naugatuck is like that.

The driver drops us off at the student center, and we have to
walk to our classes in separate buildings.

"Are you sure you're all right?" I hand her four cigarettes and a
spare lighter.

Lifting her chin, she nods. "I wish I could be tough like you," she says. "My mother's from the Bronx."

"Don't beat yourself up." I touch her arm. "You're sweet, which is refreshing in this dirty ass world. I'm 'hood enough for both of us."

She laughs. "Thanks, Livvie."

I walk to class, hoping I did the right thing by not getting the cops involved.

THERE ISN'T MUCH of a chance for me to think about Cliff until I finally stop for lunch. I head to the student center, not bothering with Conn Hall. Sometimes the food there is good, but the mall-style cafeteria in the student center has pizza, soup, and subs—exactly the kind of comfort food I need. It wasn't my car that was attacked, but my nerves are still shot.

Mostly because last night *might've* been a huge mistake.

Not the sex. I'm learning quickly that sex with Cliff is better than dropping Molly. It's the emotional side of things that has me conflicted. Even though I had to kick him out, I didn't want him to leave. Mostly I wanted to snuggle up in his arms and fall asleep like that, which is completely preposterous. Even if Lucy said she doesn't want to know, the rest of our family is going to be ultra weird about it.

If, that is, we actually dated.

Because we're not.

This is all purely hypothetical.

I *don't* date.

I buy three slices of pepperoni pizza, load them up with grated cheese and red pepper flakes, and carry them to an empty booth. Then I wall myself off from the crowd and would-be booth crashers, spreading out open books and notebooks across the table in front of me. It's an aesthetic that says, "I'm binge studying while I stuff my face between classes, so fuck off."

Really I'm just thinking about Cliff.

I'm thinking ridiculous things, like strapping a picnic basket to that motorcycle of his in the spring, or taking him to the swimming quarry when it finally gets hot enough. These are girlfriend/boyfriend thoughts, and completely against my rules. I have to be realistic and honest.

I'm graduating in just a few months. After I walk across that stage, I have to get my shit together and find a job, but that doesn't require the same amount of focus that getting through college does. Maybe there's room in my life for a boyfriend.

For Cliff.

Of course, there's no way it's going to happen. Even if he wasn't my non-cousin, he's got that whole lone wolf vibe going. Then there's the club to think about.

The little I know about MCs comes from TV, trashy novels, and rumors flying around town and the rest of the Valley. We have several clubs around here, most of which are ninety-nine-percenters. But they don't bother you as long as you don't mess with them. Hell, when I took the job at The Wet Mermaid, I had no clue that it was run by the River Reapers. I was just looking for something in town that allowed me to go to class during the day. The tips were a huge pro, and Mark hired me on the spot.

All of the guys have been good to me, but I've always just been an outsider. Everything would change if Cliff and I became a thing. I'm not really sure I want to get involved, especially since part of my job is going to be taking kids from criminals' homes. Not that the River Reapers are really into much crime. Practically everyone in this area is a drug dealer or knows one. The cops basically ignore the strip club because it's not like we're selling heroin. But it won't look good on my resume if I'm a former employee of a strip club *and* someone's ol' lady.

I put down my half-finished third slice and sigh. For the first time, I notice Eli sitting across from me. I point a glare at him. "Can't you see I'm studying?"

"Sorry," Eli says. "You looked so deep in thought, I didn't want to disturb you." He nods to the books on the table. "Exam?"

Getting up, I toss my garbage into a nearby bin and put my tray in the return receptacle. "No," I reply, sinking back into the booth. The irony of the whole thing doesn't escape me. I rub my cheeks, and decide not to mention Cliff, considering how he deliberately rubbed last night in Eli's face. "Just trying to catch up."

He watches me with hooded eyes. "Late night?"

I study him too. Eli is handsome, and sweet enough to trust me with one of his cameras, I muse, noticing the zipped bag on the table. Plus, he isn't involved in a fucking motorcycle club. My mother always told Lucy and me to make smart choices. Eli is potential boyfriend material—if I were the type of person who did that sort of thing. I smile, shaking my head. "I've just been busy with work and roommate shit." I nod to the bag. "Is that for me?"

His whole face lights up. He slides it toward me. "It's not the best, but it'll get you through the class."

"You're totally saving my ass here," I tell him. "I should've had one of my own weeks ago." Patting the case, I assure him that I'll take good care of it. "I owe you one, Eli."

He rubs his lower lip as if considering something. The T-shirt he's wearing hugs his biceps, and I trace the tattoos curling around the muscles with appreciation. He's not as big as Cliff, but he's built, and looks fun enough for a night. Maybe even more.

"Can I ask you for a favor?" His hazel eyes glint.

"Please," I tell him. "Like I said, I owe you one."

"This is so awkward." He looks away, a sandy strand of hair falling into those eyes. "I'm really stuck here, though, Olivia." His eyes meet mine.

"Okay." I shrug. "What do you need?"

"Well, I'm actually a photographer." Thick fingers pass me a business card over the table: Elijah Moretti Photography. "I'm supposed to be doing a shoot for *So Lit Couture* magazine."

My eyes widen. "Eli, that's huge!" *So Lit Couture* is another one of those online magazines that popped up in the early 2010s and took off almost overnight. It's aimed at women my age, and their fashion predictions and advice is always dead on. They don't have a print edition but I read it religiously on my laptop. Every college girl with a pulse does.

He nods, but his shoulders slump. "It is. Unfortunately my model has the flu, so she can't do it. My deadline is in two days." Eli shakes his head. "I can't find anyone else. I know it's a lot to ask, especially in exchange for a damn camera, but I was wondering—"

"Of course I'll do it," I interrupt. "A chance to be in *So Lit Couture*? Eli, you're talking about giving me eternal bragging rights."

"Well," he says slowly, "it's a bit more interesting than that."

I wait for him to elaborate, but the longer the silence stretches, the more shades of red he turns. "It's a nude shoot, isn't it?"

The strawberry color of his cheeks and forehead is all the answer I need.

I bite my lower lip to keep from laughing. "Eli, you dirty boy!"

The flat look he gives me reminds me that he's a professional.

I clear my throat. "Right. Sorry."

"It's for an article about the recent boudoir trend." He lifts a hand. "And I'd compensate you, of course."

"I'm in," I tell him. "I'm so in." Grinning, I glance down at my figure. "I guess I'm done with pizza for the next couple days."

"There is one little catch," he adds, his voice strangely flat.

I tilt my head at him.

Leaning forward, he places both elbows on the table. "I wanted to do something different." As he talks, his hands fly around. His excitement is contagious. "Boudoir is almost always indoors, and it just has that intimate feel to it. Whenever you see outdoor boudoir photography, it's still pretty, but it's lost that intimacy." His gaze is so intense, his eyes practically penetrate into mine, making me more than a little uncomfortable.

Suddenly I understand why Cliff doesn't like him. Eli is a little too fervid, almost unsettlingly so. When he first mentioned the shoot, I assumed it'd be in a studio or something, but the calculating wheels turning in his eyes are like warning bells.

My gut twists. Those empty eyes bore into me as if he's etching a target onto my forehead. Shifting in my seat, I zero in on the feeling in my stomach. It's as real as the building I'm standing in. If nothing else, I've learned to trust my instincts, because they're almost always right.

He wants me, and he's totally playing me.

Modeling for him in the woods will not end well.

I sigh. He seemed so normal, someone I might be friends with. Even though I can handle myself, there's no sense in putting myself in that position.

"You know what, Eli," I say, gathering my books, "I just remembered I took an extra shift at work. So unfortunately, I can't fill in for your model." I give him my most apologetic smile. "But check with Professor Biello. I'm sure he knows lots of models who would kill for this chance."

The blank, burning stare that Eli gives me is confirmation that my gut is right.

"Eli?" I ask, zipping my books into my bag. I move my hand to the pouch that carries the mace. I doubt that he'd try anything right in the middle of the student center, but a girl just never knows.

But his face brightens and he nods. "Yeah, you're right. Thanks." He stands. "I've got class. I'll see you later."

I hold up a hand in parting, watching him go. Only when I'm sure he's gone do I stand.

~

I'VE DEALT with men like Eli before. It's sort of been a theme in my life. Somewhere inside of me is a creeper magnet. Ever since first grade, men have been trying to dominate or scare me. And they almost always get away with it.

First there was Alex, my class partner. Everyone's desks were paired in twos and, while the rest of our class worked on addition, Alex pulled his pants down and kept trying to get me to touch him. He'd grab my hand and I'd yank my arm away, hissing for him to leave me alone.

But I never told, because I wasn't entirely sure I wouldn't get into trouble, too.

Eventually our teacher broke us up. I think she sensed that he was bothering me, but since I wouldn't say either way, she took it upon herself.

That was the last time another person ever intervened.

There was Chad in third grade, who liked to slam into me during recess. I'd sit on the stone benches outside, daydreaming or reading, and Chad would tackle me. The palms of my hands were often raw from scraping against that bench.

Chad disappeared not long after. Rumors flew around saying he raped his sister in the girls' bathroom, but this was out of the mouths of seven- and eight-year-olds, so who knows.

In seventh grade there was Jonathan feeling me up in the halls between classes, and Richard making fun of my nose and calling me a lesbian during classes. He punched me in the arm once, right in front of our Italian teacher. But because I swore in pain, I'm the one who got detention.

On and on it goes. I'm a serial victim, so Eli is no surprise. The only difference is, since graduating high school, I've learned how to deal with assholes like him. I'm more worried about paying for Esther's tires.

I could be wrong, but I think the mysterious visitor and the tire slasher were Eli.

During my next class, I sit in the back crunching numbers. I've been putting the majority of my strip club money into repaying my student debt, with the rest going into paying bills. Some of it goes into a savings account. If I cut down on groceries and go without Netflix for a few months, I can buy Esther new tires immediately. I don't know what to do about her keyed trunk, though.

My phone vibrates in my pocket. Glancing around to make sure I'm not disturbing anyone, I peer at the screen.

It's Cliff, who's apparently learned how to text. I can't hide the goofy grin that spreads across my face. My little alien has learned how to use an iPhone just for me.

Cliff: Is it cool if I pick you up from school?

Every word is in perfect English—either he hasn't learned any of the abbreviations or slang yet, or he's too cool to use any of it. I mentally swoon a little harder.

Still, the weather bursts my bubble. It's cold again, and the roads were slick with melting snow, which froze over. Fucking Connecticut. I text back, matching his precise grammar.

Olivia: Are you going to fly?

The phone vibrates in my hand—an incoming call.

He's actually *calling* me.

Too thrilled to notice whether anyone is annoyed with me, I practically skip out of class and into the hall.

I take a deep breath before answering, so that I don't sound as pleased as I feel. "Hey," I say, my voice casual. Only my heart jackhammering in my chest betrays the emotions swirling through me. *He called, he called, he called*, my heart drums out.

"Hey," Cliff replies, his voice sounding as cool and smoky as usual. "Am I interrupting you?"

Just my field practice seminar lecture, which is fancy college slang for internship. I wasn't paying attention, anyway. I bite back a giggle. "I was just doing some math."

"Ooh," he says, that husky voice making his grimace sound even sexier. "Fun."

"Like having your fingernails ripped out," I agree, leaning against a wall. "So what's up?"

"I wanted to see you." No bullshit. Just exactly what's on his mind. It's refreshing, and arousing as hell.

Suddenly I don't care about the icy roads or the rest of my classes for the day. I know I should, since I've already missed so much and I need to finish up my field work hours so that I can graduate. But every cell in me wants to jump on that bike with him and escape.

Still, that would be the opposite of playing hard to get. If I'm going to pursue this boyfriend/girlfriend thing—or at least entertain the idea—I can't just jump every time he asks me out.

I blink. He's asking me out, and I'm about to turn him down.

"Olivia?" That low, gravelly voice sends warm shivers all the way down to my toes.

I sag against the wall. "You're killing me," I breathe.

"The suspense is killing *me*." He laughs. "So are we on?"

Sighing, I straighten. "I can't. I have to adult," I say, thinking of the mountain of phone calls I need to make. Tires, field work placement, oh my. Then I really do have a shift at The Wet Mermaid.

"Hmn." Even that tiny syllable sends vibrations of lust rippling through me. "Well, I'm working tonight. Can we do something after?"

What I like most about Cliff, I realize, is how he's just dominating enough to be protective and sexy, without being overbearing and disgusting. He respects my boundaries and needs.

Even if I'm uncertain about pursuing, there's one thing about Cliff that I am sure about: he'll never force himself on me. If I tell him to, he'll walk away without looking back.

"Yes," I say, even though I have class early in the morning. And speaking of class, I'm probably missing something important. It's time to put my adult hat back on. "I've got to go."

"Hold on. Do you need a ride into work?"

"I do," I reply, drawing out the word, "but it's kind of icy out."

He chuffs. "We can take Lucy's car, you know."

My mind flashes to the station wagon, and my cheeks burn. "Right." It would be so wrong to mess around with Cliff in my sister's car. It'd also be incredibly cramped, considering how small her car is and how big he is. Heat shoots through me to my lower abdomen, every muscle inside of me clenching. There's just something incredibly hot about a guy who's three or four times my size but likes to cuddle after sex. Regret burrows into me from kicking him out the other night.

"I'll pick you up at your place for 6:30. Cool?"

"Cool," I breathe.

It takes me several minutes to de-Jello my legs and get both my heart rate and libido under control. In just three weeks, I've gone from hit and run to seriously considering pursuing whatever it is that Cliff and I have. The prospect is both terrifying and thrilling—mostly because I have no idea whether we're both interested in the same things.

There's only one way to find out, though.

11

CLIFF

"So," Lucy asks, strapping herself into the passenger seat, "what's going on between you and my little sister?"

The way she says *my little sister* is so fiercely protective, I glance at her. The expression on her face is just as fierce, her brows furrowed, eyes slits that imply a threat behind the words. And I believe it.

"I thought you didn't want to know," I reply, treading carefully. My hands grip the steering wheel, and I wish that we could just get on with it. Asking Lucy for a refresher course on driving a car involved way more pride swallowing than I'd bargained for. It's not that she was mean or anything. I just feel like a loser.

Lucy taps her lower lip. "I guess I don't. But I also do." She twists in her seat to face me. "Does that make sense?"

"Of course it does." I glance around the industrial park. Too many memories here. Ironically enough, it was my father who taught me how to drive when I was fifteen. I just never got my license.

"Just promise me something," Lucy continues. "Be . . . careful with Olivia. She's not really the settle down and get married type."

I snort. "And you are?"

"Of course not." She scowls. "But you are, and Livvie breaks hearts for a living."

Smirking, I cock my head at her. "How do you know I'm all about the hearts and flowers?"

"You kissed my fucking boo-boos when I was like three, dude." Lucy's green eyes pin me. "And you had the biggest crush on that girl that lived next door to you. Said you were gonna marry her someday."

Violet. I nod, remembering. "I was a kid, Luce."

"So you're telling me you just want to bang my sister and leave her hanging?" The glare she skewers me with is so badass, it's funny.

But I don't laugh. I get the feeling this conversation is important to Lucy. It's similar to a "What are your intentions, son?" talk with a father. I sigh. "I don't know, Luce." I spread my hands. "I like her, but . . ."

She lifts both eyebrows, encouraging me to continue.

There are no words to explain how I'm feeling. Olivia frustrates me, in a good way. A dangerously good way. I probably don't need that in my life right now. My priorities should be keeping my P.O. happy and making sure the MC isn't dragging me into the one-percent life. Wedding bells and babies are not one of those priorities. I try to picture Olivia in a white dress.

The image is so good, it shocks me.

I hurry to light a cigarette, shaking my head. "She should stay away from me, Luce," I say softly, staring at the empty parking lot through the windshield.

"No." The single word is forceful.

I turn to look at my cousin, confused. One minute she's interrogating me, the next she's upset that I want Olivia to stay away. "Why the hell not?"

"Because," she says, "you look good together. I have a feeling about you two."

Now I laugh. "Yeah? Because your feelings are so dead on."

"I was right about you," she says, her voice small.

I freeze, the laughter dying on my lips.

"No one else wanted to help me. But I knew you would protect me. You promised, remember?" She grabs my hand, giving me a gentle smile.

Nodding, I suck in a deep breath. "Luce, you don't have to talk about it."

"But I do. I remember everything." Her grip on my hand tightens. "I told my parents, and they didn't believe me. So then I told you."

This story is too familiar. I already know how it ends. And *I* don't want to talk about it, I realize. Because deep down, some part of me resents Lucy. I bow my head.

"It's okay," she whispers. "I know. And it's okay."

I glance up at her. The emotions swimming in her eyes must mirror mine. I swallow hard. "It's not okay," I force out. "Because it wasn't an accident."

She bites her lip. "You did what you had to do."

"I thought I was doing it for you." Blinking, I see a flash of the past, Lucy huddled in the corner of the kitchen, those green eyes locked on mine. Her face pale, small body shaking in shock. And me, towering over my father's lifeless body, his blood still hot and wet on my hands. I hadn't even hesitated. There was no question. "I liked it, Luce. I was high on it." Even though I'm looking at the adult sitting next to me, all I can see is the little girl in the kitchen with the monster standing in front of her. "And I hurt you," I finish, lifting the cigarette to my lips with shaking fingers.

She scoffs. "You didn't *hurt* me. I was scared. And I'd never seen anything . . . like that before." She squeezes my hand again. "Cliff, you *saved* me. He would've done it again and again. And no one else was going to stop him. I sure as fuck couldn't." Green eyes tug me back into the present, back from the edge.

"I shoved you into that cabinet," I say between gritted teeth. "If the cops hadn't come—"

Her gaze holds me. "You didn't shove me. You were trying to keep me safe from him." She shakes her head. "Jesus, Cliff. Why are you making yourself out to be the bad guy? I was there, too. And I know you. I know what I saw."

I don't know why I expected her to understand. She can't possibly feel what I do. Only when you become the monster do you understand the power that comes with taking a life. It's still there, whispering to me.

"It was so easy." I finish the cigarette, flicking it out the window. "He didn't even beg, didn't even apologize. Sometimes I wonder if I still would've done it."

"There's no point in torturing yourself," Lucy says. "What's done is done. All you can do is continue being a good man. Because you *are*, Cliff. You doubt yourself, but I've never doubted who you are. You're not the bad guy in this story."

This conversation is just depressing. I thought Lucy was the only person in the world who understands me, but she doesn't know me at all. It's just another wedge between us.

I shift the car into drive. "Thanks, Luce." One corner of my mouth lifts in what I hope is a convincing smile. "All right, kid. Teach me how to drive."

We spend the next hour brushing me up on the basics. It's muscle memory, really, because soon I'm zipping around the empty lot. Parallel parking is the only thing I can't do, but I never nailed it as a teenager, either. Lucy shows me a trick for backing into spaces, assuring me that I'll definitely pass my driver's license test.

"As long as they forget to have you parallel park," she says.

"Thanks for the vote of confidence."

"Just being honest." She pats my shoulder. "All right, take us home."

It's not the same as riding a hog, but I handle the car well enough, bringing us back to Lucy's condo in one piece. Part of me wonders if it's even worth getting a driver's license. All I want to do is ride. But Lucy and even most of my new brothers agree that if I'm going to go legit, I might as well get both.

"That was smooth," Lucy compliments me as we pull into her driveway. "So where are you taking Livvie tonight?"

I grunt. "Just work. Then maybe somewhere after. I don't know." I peek at her out of the corner of one eye. "Where *should* I take her?"

She covers a smile with her hand. "That late at night?" She lifts an eyebrow at me.

I slump back in my seat. "Straight home, I guess."

"Good boy." Planting a quick kiss on my cheek, she unbuckles her seatbelt. "Behave, kids." She slides out and waves goodbye, then disappears inside.

I head to Olivia's, 99.1 PLR's broadcast of songs I grew up with cranking out of the speakers as I navigate the back roads to avoid being pulled over. It's a bit unnerving, knowing that music from my childhood is now considered classic rock. The world moved on while I was inside.

I pull up in front of her apartment, the engine idling while I try to decide whether to get out and knock on the door. It would be the gentlemanly thing to do, but I don't know whether we're dating. I don't know what we're doing at all.

I get out anyway and jog up to the front door. A tiny meow greets me from the other side, giving me away. I knock and then back off a couple steps. I don't want to look too eager.

The door swings open a crack. A Puerto Rican woman wearing nothing but a bathrobe peers out at me. She's about Olivia's age, and the look on her face is suspicious at best. "Who the fuck are you?"

I open my mouth to answer, but Olivia marches up behind the other woman.

"It's just Cliff," she says, grinning at me.

Her roommate opens the door all the way, scowling the whole time, but she moves aside so I can come in.

Olivia hugs me with one arm, an orange furball tucked into the crook of her other arm. She lifts a hand toward her roommate. "This is Esther."

I nod at Esther. "Nice to meet you."

She *hmph*s and stalks away into her bedroom.

"Not very friendly, huh?" I nod toward Esther's room.

"Esther? She's just having a bad day," Olivia says. She holds the kitten out to me. "This is Dio."

Dio sniffs at my hand, then gives my fingers a hearty rub. Instant friendship. I scratch behind an ear.

Olivia pushes him into my arms. "Get to know each other. I just need to finish getting ready." She disappears into her bedroom.

Standing in the middle of the kitchenette, I exchange bro looks with Dio. "That's code for 'I'll be out in an hour.'" I carry him to the futon. He stretches out belly up in my lap, eyes imploring me to get rubbing. This cat is more dog than anything else. I oblige, absently scratching under his chin and stroking his tiny belly. A loud purr vibrates from him, and a laugh escapes my lips. "You got any brothers or sisters, Dio?" Lucy's is quiet and empty during the day. I could use the company.

Olivia emerges a few minutes later. The dark jeans she's wearing hug her curves, her cream colored sweater snug around her hips and breasts. It's going to be really hard to just drop her off at home and then leave tonight.

"Ready?" She lifts Dio from my lap and plants a kiss on the soft spot between his eyes. "No wild parties, okay?" She releases him onto the floor, where he chases a catnip mouse that's almost as big as he is.

Linking arms with me, she calls out "Have a good night!" to Esther and tugs me out the door.

"There's a diner open 24/7," she says as we walk to the car. "I figured maybe we can grab something there after work?"

My shoulders relax. I don't have to write off the night with her, after all. "Cool."

The drive to The Wet Mermaid is short, but the silence between us is comfortable. Familiar. I park in the back and shut off the engine, listening to it tick as the car cools. I should probably say something boyfriend-like, test the waters. But I don't know what to say. Lucy is right—Olivia is as independent as a cat. I don't want to scare her away.

"We'd better go in," Olivia says, pushing open her door.

I follow her inside, but Beer Can flags me down.

"Can you start right now?" he asks, grimacing. "I've gotta piss."

Nodding, I let him go. I watch Olivia set up her station, chatting with a few regulars who are already lit for the night. The smile she gives them is friendly but guarded. It's not the same open smile that she gives me.

Or maybe I'm kidding myself.

All throughout the night, I can barely take my eyes off her. The way she tucks those wild curls behind a tiny ear. How she nods politely while strangers tell her about their troubles. Olivia is a good girl. She has no business being with someone like me.

I have to let her go.

Finally we close. My responsibilities are technically done with for the night, but I'm still her ride home, despite what I've decided. I help wipe down tables and put up chairs. There's a sullen energy in the air. It's not just me who feels it.

Several of my brothers pour themselves after-hours drinks and head to Church. Something is up with the club, but as a Prospect, I'm not privy to it. Frowning, I watch the stragglers trickle in. Vinny is the last one in, and he closes the door behind him with a heavy thud. My frown deepens.

"I'm all punched out." Olivia bumps my hip with hers as she joins me. "Ready?"

I nod toward the door. "Any idea what's going on?"

She nibbles on her lower lip. "Just club business. Why?"

Shrugging, I lean against the wall. "I don't know. Just have a bad feeling."

Her faces scrunches up. "So serious." She grabs my hand. "Come on. Let's get out of here and enjoy what's left of the night before they make us mop or something."

Lips pressed together, I follow her out to the car. The night is quiet, heavy like my thoughts. I start the engine, already regretting my decision. It's for her own good. I have to remember that.

"Just a heads up, the diner's food is really, really bad," Olivia says with a laugh. "But it's the only choice we've got."

I say nothing and head toward her apartment. Part of me screams to turn around, to go to the diner like we'd planned. But what kind of man would I be if I dragged someone like Olivia into this life?

My hands clench around the steering wheel.

"Cliff," Olivia says, puzzled. "The diner's in the opposite direction."

My jaw tightens. I have to keep my resolve.

"We're not going out, are we." It's a statement, not a question, her voice full of dejection.

It occurs to me that she wanted this just as much as I did.

"Fuck," I say, and swing into a side street. When I glance over at her, she's grinning.

"You can't say no to me." She laughs.

"That's half my problem," I reply, guiding the car toward the diner. It's an old restaurant—one that was around ages before I was put away. I don't tell her that I've been to the Athenian II a million times before, that it was a popular post-prom hangout when I was in high school. It was also a good place to get food after a party in the woods got busted.

I grin. I have a lot of great memories of this place, and it seems it's time to add one more.

When I pull into the parking lot, though, it's immediately obvious that something isn't right. Weeds poke up through the cracks in the pavement. The big sign outside, yellow with age and weather, is unlit. All of the windows are dark, too.

"Well, shit," Olivia says. "I never thought I'd see the day."

"I guess all of those health code violations finally caught up to them." I laugh.

"What are we gonna do now?"

I bite back a dirty suggestion. Glancing across the street, I spot a Taco Bell.

She follows my gaze. "Oh no. We had enough of that shit in Pennsylvania."

Tucking my upper lip into my lower one, I pout, giving her sad brown eyes.

"Don't play the ex-con card with me. Do you even know what's in that shit?"

I deepen the puppy face.

"I really wanted ice cream." She sighs, eyeing the closed diner longingly. "McDonald's over on Lakewood has ice cream . . ." She wiggles her eyebrows at me.

I pretend to consider it, a corner of my mouth lifting in deep thought. "Big Mac or Crunchwrap," I ponder out loud.

She swats me in the arm and chants "Ice cream, ice cream!"

Grinning, I maneuver the car out of the diner's overgrown parking lot and head toward McDonald's. It's right on the next street over, so it really isn't a big deal. Plus, it doesn't interrupt our plans. Despite how much I know I should walk away, I can't deny how I feel.

I get a Big Mac and a giant McFlurry with M&Ms for my little ice cream junkie, and we share a large fry and soda. I pull into the dim back lot behind the Taco Bell plaza and we munch in silence. Everything with her is so comfortable and easy. It can't stay that way forever. Sooner or later, I'll have to choose. Or she will.

Olivia is going to be a social worker. I know which choice she'll make.

"So," she says after she's put away that giant ice cream. She lights two cigarettes and passes one to me.

I'm so full, I can barely move. "I should probably lay off the fast food, but it's so good. They must put crack in it."

She laughs. "Something like that."

We smoke in silence for several long beats. Then she turns to me, putting a hand on my arm. She takes a deep breath.

"Cliff," she says.

I cock my head and nod for her to go on. Amusement flickers in her eyes at the gesture, and I laugh out loud. "You can take the man out of prison, but you can't take prison out of the man."

She bobs her head. "Yeah, I know." Pressing her lips together, she seems to be considering something.

"Just lay it out," I tell her. "It's you and me."

"Yeah," she says slowly, "that's kind of the thing." She taps ash out the window. "Look, I'm sure you're in no rush. I mean, I thought I wasn't. But I'm kind of wondering—you know, no pressure—well . . ." Those luminous eyes latch onto mine. "What are we doing here, Cliff?"

My first inclination is to state the obvious. I know she means more than that, though. "What do *you* think we're doing?" I ask, my voice gentle.

She bites her lip. "When you called me today, I guess I kind of thought you were asking me out." She sucks in her cheeks, eyes widening. "But if I was wrong, I'm sorry," she says quickly.

"I'm not really sure what I'm doing, Liv." I sigh, tipping my head back. Suddenly the car is too hot. I shut the heat off. This is the part where I tell her we can't be together, that twice was enough. This has to stop. But I don't want to.

Whatever that means, I'll figure it out, dealing with the consequences as we go.

I can't express this to her without sounding like a total loser. I clench one hand in and out of a fist, flexing the small muscles. I'm smoking a cigarette but I need a damn stress ball.

I lick my lips. Turning toward her, I look her straight in the eyes. Let her see me. *Really* see me. Past the prison facade, the Prospect vest. I just have to hope she doesn't see the monster.

"I don't want to stop," I tell her, my voice thick.

Something in her eyes flare, hopes fulfilled. She grabs the back of my neck and pulls me toward her, her lips crushing against mine. "I don't want to, either," she whispers into my mouth.

Then she releases me, just as quickly as the kiss was ignited. I'm left panting in the driver's seat, hard and ready, heart thrumming. "Christ, Olivia," I growl.

She smirks at me. "I have to be at school early in the morning. I have a meeting with my professor to set up my field work." She rolls her eyes. "I'm a little behind."

I close my eyes. "Because of Lewisburg?" I can't be fucking up her life already.

"No." She scoffs. "Because I was too busy getting laid and not making phone calls like I was supposed to."

Fuckin' A. My girl is a hundred times more experienced than me. The realization should make me jealous, but it only turns me on. I want her dominating me, teacher to student. I lean forward, eager to capture those lips in mine again.

She twirls a finger at me. "Uh-uh. Take me home, please."

"Tomorrow night?" I ask, grinning. I'm so hooked on this girl, we could read The Babysitter's Club books to each other for all I care. As long as we end up naked somewhere in between. I want to know everything about her, to learn what she likes and hates.

She taps her lips. "Maybe."

But I catch the smile underneath the pad of her finger, and I know she's just as hooked on me as I am on her.

12

OLIVIA

Cliff's lips press to mine, an exchange of warmth. He smiles against my lips. I can't help but smile back. I step away, though, the late night tugging me toward bed. I really do have an early morning ahead of me, but it helps to play hard to get. If I'm going to do this—really do this—I'm going to do it right.

As right as I can, anyway.

Sliding him one last smile, I unlock my door and step inside. Cliff drives away as I close the door behind me. I lock it and lean against it, still smiling. If someone ever figures out how to bottle this feeling, they're going to be rich.

The apartment is mostly dark, lit only by a lamp in the living room area. Esther is either still at work, or out with her new boyfriend Donny. He picked her up earlier, since she still has no tires. He's nice—I get why she likes him. Tall with deep bronzed skin, he has a kind smile, but there's a bad boy edge to him. Something in those eyes. The guy could be a model.

I hum to myself as I make my way through the apartment. Esther and me, the two most unlikely people to ever fall in love. I stop in my tracks, shaking my head.

No, no. *Not* love.

"Damn it, Olivia," I mutter.

I correct myself as I push open my bedroom door. We're the two most unlikely women to ever settle down into actual relationships.

There.

The smile slides from my face as I flick on the switch.

Bright light floods my bedroom, but the only thing I can see is blood

so much blood

on my bed

and a tiny, matted form underneath all of it.

I rush over to Dio, but hesitate over him. Mumbles of protest tumble from my lips, tears blurring my vision. Mascara and eyeliner sting into my eyes. I cup my hands, bending over the kitten. My fingers and palms shake on my wrists like loose leaves on a tree branch.

"No, no, no," I whisper in a strangled, breathy voice that isn't mine.

I don't know the first thing about first aid for a human, never mind a tiny ball of life and laughter. I'm afraid to move him, but I don't know what else to do.

My mind whirls. I can't breathe. Sinking to my knees, I can't look away from Dio. I rock back and forth on the floor, panting and grunting.

One of Dio's eyes cracks open. He utters a short, plaintive mewl. Then his eye closes again.

My heart shatters into pieces, the sensation jerking me into action. I pull my phone out of my bag and dial the first number that comes to mind.

"911, what's your emergency?" a calm, bored sounding woman asks.

"My cat," I sputter. "Someone broke into my house and—"

The phone drops from my hands.

A chill crawls down my spine, traveling through my legs.

Eli.

I glance around, checking the window in my bedroom. It's intact, still locked, even. I start to move toward the living room, to check the other windows, when the dispatcher's sharp voice brings me back to what's important.

Dio.

I grab the phone and press it to my ear, and pace the room.

"Ma'am, is there someone in your house?" the dispatcher asks.

"I don't think so. Not anymore," I stammer. "But my cat, he's hurt, he's been attacked—"

"Okay, ma'am, you need to take your animal to a vet." Through the phone, I hear her typing on a computer. "I can give you the phone number to the closest twenty-four-hour emergency animal hospital."

"Okay." I swallow several times to coat my dry throat. Then I grab a pen off my dresser, poising it over the palm of my hand.

The dispatcher rattles off the phone number. "Ma'am, if you're more comfortable with me sending a patrol car over, I can certainly—"

"I need to get him to the hospital," I sob, and hang up.

I call the emergency vet, who sounds like a grandfather who was dead asleep. Small wonder, since it's just about four in the morning. He walks me through picking up Dio, telling me I probably don't need to put him in his carrier.

"But Olivia?" The vet says my name hesitantly.

"Yes?" I choke out, searching for a clean T-shirt to wrap Dio in.

"I wouldn't rush, sweetheart. It's probably too late." His voice is too kind.

"Don't say that," I snarl through a fresh stream of tears. "I'll be there in ten minutes. Get dressed and do your fucking job." I hang up on him and throw my phone into my bag.

Then I turn to Dio.

My stomach clenches. Moving him could be the last straw.

Tears continue gushing down my cheeks. I choke back another sob and get to it. Being a baby about it isn't going to save him.

I place a thick, soft sweater on a shoebox lid. The sweater was his favorite. He loved kneading on it.

I scrunch up my face.

Is.

Loves.

He's not gone yet.

Gently, I slide the lid underneath him inch by inch. He doesn't even protest. His tiny body rises and falls in rapid jerks. My heart breaks again and again.

"I'm sorry," I soothe. "You're gonna be okay, Dio. Just hang on. I'm here. I'm here."

When I finally have the lid all the way underneath him, I tuck the sweater around him. Then, grabbing my bag, I pick him up as carefully as possible.

I hurry outside, the blast of cold air clarifying my thoughts. As I stand on the front walk, I realize I have no car.

My eyes close in despair.

A war wages within me. There's no time to call an Uber. And there's no one I can call. No one, I realize, except Cliff. But he's at least ten minutes away, which tacks on twenty minutes to the veterinary hospital. I glance up and down the street in desperation. I can jack a car. It can't be that hard.

I start toward one. As I'm crossing the street, headlights flood my vision. I stop dead on the double yellow line, wondering if Eli's come to finish the job.

"Olivia?" Esther calls out the passenger window. "What's wrong? What are you—? Oh god."

Donny hits the brakes, but Esther's out before the car is even fully stopped.

"Get in," she says, shooing me into the back seat, her eyes filling with tears.

I hug Dio in my lap the entire way over. Everything in me

wants to rock back and forth, to sooth myself. But it's all I can to do keep him stable as Donny attempts to navigate the potholes that pock every inch of the Naugatuck streets. He pushes the car until he's doing sixty, in an attempt to get us to the Waterbury address in under ten minutes. None of us speak.

Somehow Dio holds on. I fling open the door and rush him inside.

"Please save him," I whimper as I hand him over to the veterinarian's assistant.

She gives me a sympathetic look. "We'll do our best," she says, but I know that face. I press a stack of crisp twenty-dollar bills into another staff member's hands—everything I have. Fuck Esther's tires. I've got to save my cat.

Donny, Esther, and I huddle in the parking lot, chainsmoking and glancing through the window every ten seconds, as if we can see straight through the walls into the operating room.

"Olivia, what happened?" Esther asks after I've smoked my way through my pack.

I tell her everything, filling her in on how I figured out that Eli was the one who slit her tires. I'd texted her earlier to tell her that Donny wasn't the problem, that I had my own stalker. But I hadn't had the chance to catch her up.

When I'm done, I'm exhausted. I sag against Donny's car, limp. My mind keeps flashing to Dio, crumpled on my bed.

"Who the fuck would do this to a little cat?" Donny seethes, echoing my thoughts.

I glance up at him. For the first time, I notice that he's wearing a River Reapers cut. His badge reads ENFORCER. I really look at his face. Then I recognize him.

I don't see him often. He's usually out on club business. Or, apparently, working with my roommate. Every once in a while he stops in to The Wet Mermaid, mostly for Church. When he does order a drink, which is rare, he tips me excessively well.

"Donny," I ask slowly, "what is it that you do for the club?"

His jaw tightens, his lips clamping shut.

Pushing off the car, I stride up to him. I clasp my hands together. "Donny, please. I need to talk to Mark. I *know*," I tell him.

"Christ," he swears, rubbing his temples. He lights a cigarette, glances at my empty hands, then tosses me his pack.

Esther reaches for it, too, her eyes wide and haunted. Guilt scrapes at my stomach. Because of me, my mousey roommate's sense of safety has been rattled. I wrap an arm around her waist, and she rests her head on my shoulder.

"Donny," I say, my eyes burning into him. "I'm everybody's bartender. I know about the guns." I don't know what's on my face. If it's anything like what I'm feeling, it's raw desperation. I lift my chin. "I need one, Donny. I need a gun. I need to talk to Mark—"

"Okay," he hisses, glancing around. "Hush, woman." He gives his head a shake.

Still wrapped in one of my arms, Esther hugs herself. Her forehead creases, and she chews on the inside of her cheek.

Donny presses a flip phone to his ear—a burner. "Mark," he says. "I've got a situation." He shoots us a look that tells us to stay put, then steps several paces out of earshot.

I'm too pumped up with adrenaline to realize that he barely put up an argument. The club has always given me special treatment, so I'm pretty used to it. Still, Donny's fast yes is almost unnerving.

I hug Esther tighter.

"I hope he isn't going to tell Cliff," I mutter.

"Why the fuck not, pendeja?" She curls her lip. "If I were you, I'd have him stomp in that motherfucker's head." Her face pales. "How the fuck did he get in, anyway?"

I move my head back and forth. I don't know. I just know one thing: I'm going to kill him. I don't know where or when, but I am. It's one thing to follow me to class or key my roommate's car.

Those are the oldest tricks in the stalkers' guide for dummies. But now he's overstepped his bounds.

My blood boils as I move away from Esther. I exhale a cloud of smoke and walk through it toward Donny. He leans against his car, arms crossed. Watching me, a look of awe on his face.

"How come you're not on your bike?" I ask him.

He blinks, surprised by my question. "Because the roads are shit right now."

"But the rest of the club rides year-round." I hug myself against the cold. The shock is wearing off.

"No, they don't, babygirl." He glances at Esther, who's playing on her phone. He nods to me. "Come around to the trunk."

When he flips open the lid, at first I only see a neatly folded blanket and some random tools. He lifts the rug-covered cardboard divider that ordinarily separates the storage space from the spare tire well. Fitted into the hole where his donut should be is a circular wooden crate.

I lift an eyebrow. "I'm already impressed."

He rolls his eyes and opens the crate, exposing rows of carefully packed handguns. "Glock 34. It's a nine millimeter," he says, lifting one from its foam padding and handing it to me.

Its weight presses into more than just my hands.

"Serial number's been filed off," Donny continues. "The kick isn't too violent, so you should be able to shoot it." His eyebrows furrow as he looks down at me. "You do know how to shoot one, right?"

It's my turn to roll my eyes. "Of course I do."

He hands me a threaded barrel. "Silencer."

"I know what it is," I say, threading it in.

"You'll need a holster. Connecticut ain't open carry."

I sigh, exasperated. "Look, Donny, I'm not brand new."

"You're so much like him," he mutters.

"Who?" I twist off the silencer.

Donny hands me several boxes of rounds. "Nobody, little one."

But this time his head shake is affectionate. "This is between you, me, and Mark. And Esther." The corner of his lips twitches in a half grimace. "Please don't shoot yourself in the foot or anything like that."

My hands are too full to put on my hips. I tilt my head instead. "Donny, my *father* taught me how to shoot." My brow furrows. I don't remember our dad ever even owning a gun, never mind taking Lucy or I to a shooting range. I hadn't thought I remembered anything about my biological parents, but maybe I do.

Putting muscle memory to test, I dam my thoughts behind a wall. My fingers do the work, loading the clip and turning a round into the chamber. I screw the silencer back on and take aim.

"See that beer can on that concrete block?" I ask Donny.

He follows my gaze.

"I'm putting one right in it."

"Right here? Out in the open, huh?" Donny crosses his arms.

I take a deep breath. Lick my lips. Then I squeeze the trigger.

The bullet flies into the can, knocking it off the construction block. The sound is so low, it's undetectable to the veterinarians working on my cat. My heart squeezes at the thought of Dio. I turn to face Donny, an eyebrow lifted.

"You just got lucky," he says, but he's smiling, almost proudly.

"Fine," I say, and scan the parking lot for something else to shoot. A tag sale poster hangs on a telephone pole. I pivot my body toward it.

"That's too easy." Donny points to a banner hanging across the street, announcing the city's message of love and hope to all who drive by. "Put a hole in the R," he says.

So I do. Every letter that he calls out.

Donny finally relents. "All right, all right. I'm impressed." He squeezes my arm gently. "But Olivia, you know all you gotta do is say the word."

My eyes snap to his. "I knew it," I say sadly.

He moves his head slightly to the side in a sort of shrug. "But you're like your daddy," he continues. "You've gotta take care of everything yourself."

I blink in response. Then I take apart my gun, put the safety on, and put it in my purse. Nestled among pens, packs of gum, and spare lighters, it fits right in.

The realization doesn't scare me at all.

In fact, it feels like I've come home.

13

CLIFF

When I wake up the next morning, the house around me is quiet. Rolling onto my side, sheets sliding against my naked body, I pat around on the nightstand for my phone. It's after ten. I haven't slept in this long in ages.

There are no missed texts or calls, but that's no surprise. Only a handful of people have my phone number. One of them is at work, another is in class, and the rest of them are probably sleeping off hangovers. I smirk, thinking of my brothers' somber faces as they headed into Church last night, drinks clutched in their hands. Someday I'll be a part of that, too.

It feels good to belong to something again.

It feels even better to belong to *someone*.

Even if Olivia and I haven't exactly called it, I feel it. Maybe it sounds sappy, but there's a connection between us that I've never felt with anyone before.

I force myself out of bed, bare feet padding across the floor. Lucy should be at work, but I pull on clothes before I leave the guest bedroom—just in case. The weather is calling for snow, so it isn't a riding lesson day. And I don't have to be at The Wet

Mermaid until later. I make coffee, feeling untethered. For the first time in twenty years, there's nowhere I have to be.

While I wait for the coffee pot to get going, I consider my options. I can surprise Olivia at school . . . but that would make me seem clingy. It's better to wait 'til we're at work. Since Lucy showed me how to download apps, I decide to camp out on the couch catching up on TV and apartment hunting. I know I'm going to break Lucy's heart the day I move out, but I need my own place—especially if Olivia and I are going to continue seeing each other.

I don't exactly smile as I carry my coffee into the living room, but it's close. Just as I go to sit down, my phone vibrates in my pocket.

I tug it out and frown as I read the display. Right. There's one more person who has my phone number: Govender, my P.O.

"Yeah," I say, slumping into the couch. This whole thing is just a pain in the ass. "Missing me already?"

"I miss you like a hemorrhoid," he says, "especially since you blew me off this morning."

I choke on my coffee. "We had a meeting?" I glance around the living room, as if expecting a calendar to appear and prove him wrong.

Govender sighs. "It's almost cute how you all try to get away with this shit." His voice grows stern. "My office. *Now*." He hangs up, the slamming of the receiver of his phone stinging my ear.

So much for my lazy morning.

I down my coffee and grab a heavy sweatshirt. I start to put my cut on over it, then hesitate. Govender may not approve. Then again, the only transportation I have is the Screamin' Eagle. It's not like my P.O. won't be able to put two and two together. Besides, I've got nothing to hide. Maybe my girlfriend—I grin at the label—sells coke from behind the bar, but I'm not doing anything wrong. All I'm doing is riding flank and keeping seventeen-year-old punks out of our strip club.

As I stride outside, I glance up at the sky, hoping the snow will hold off. The last thing I need is to get into an accident. I'm gonna have to start scheduling reminders into my phone like some businessman.

I haul ass out to Govender's office in Bristol. I'm not completely sure how this whole thing works, but I know missing a meeting with my P.O. is bad. The first flakes tumble from the sky just as I pull into the parking lot. It fucking figures.

I find Govender napping in his office.

"Christ," I mutter, knocking loudly on the open door.

He jerks up in his chair, the whites of his eyes a stark contrast to his dark skin as they open. "Well, if it isn't Clifford 'Red Dog' Demmel." He flashes white teeth at me.

This man is never vulnerable, even in his sleep.

I give him a cool look but say nothing about him using my full name. Nor am I surprised that he knows my nickname. It's slightly odd that he's using it, though. Red Dog was meant to be a joke. After I punched out some teeth and broke some ribs, though, they all stopped laughing.

I sit down, and Govender gets to business.

"You're enjoying your new job?" he asks, a pen poised above a yellow legal pad. He always takes notes during our meetings, as if he's my therapist.

Brow furrowed, I study him. My hands lay flat on my side of his desk. For a moment, I'm transported to meetings with my lawyer, the cuffs digging into my wrists. I shake the ghosts away. "Yeah," I rasp. "But I'm wondering, why did you set me up with a motorcycle club?" I have no strategy here. I'm just curious.

Govender scribbles something down. "I'm not sure I know what you're talking about, son." He peers at me with lifted eyebrows. "You're reporting for your scheduled work hours on time?"

I shift in my seat. The crease between my eyebrows remains.

"The River Reapers," I say, leaning forward. "The strip club I bounce for is owned by the River Reapers."

He cocks his head at me, looking stern in a grandfatherly way. He's about that age. "Son," he says, exasperated, "the sooner we get through this meeting, the sooner I can go back to my nap." He taps his notepad with the other end of his pen. "Now, would you say you work about forty hours a week?"

"So you're just going to pretend like this is no big deal?" I straighten the vest on my shoulders, the heavy leather creaking under my fingertips. "I'm a Prospect. For a potentially one-percent club. And you have no problem with that?"

"Forty hours, then," he says, writing something else down.

I don't know what his angle is, and it pisses me off. I stand, towering over him. "We done here?"

"Sit down." His tone is bored.

Eyes narrowing, I remain standing.

Govender stands too, his chair moving back a couple of inches on its wheels. He's not nearly as tall as I am, but he glowers up at me anyway. "Son, I'm going to give you a piece of friendly advice. You're going to shut your mouth for two minutes and take it." He places his notes and pen on the desk. "None of us can ever really grasp the inner workings of this world. When we find our places in it, we don't try to dismantle things. Do you understand?"

I don't know what the fuck that means, but I shrug. "Whatever."

We both return to our seats.

"Now, next week, I'm going to need copies of your pay stubs," he continues, as if everything about this meeting has been business as usual. "And I have here in your file that you're staying with your cousin, Ms. Lucy Demmel. What are your long-term plans for housing?"

The remainder of the meeting goes quickly, though, and soon I'm out the door, boots tracking through a light dusting of snow.

I'm starting to feel out of control again, like everyone around me is just using me in some game.

I'm not a kid. I know how the world works. But during the last twenty years, I've been playing a very different game. The rules were simple. The stakes were nearly nonexistent. In some ways, finishing out my sentence would have been better than all of this.

I swing onto the hog. Fuck the snow. I need a ride to clear my head.

I kick and take off, the machine humming between my legs. It probably says a lot that men like me need to ride something powerful in order to feel powerful. Pared down, the River Reapers are just a brotherhood of the broken. All of us are looking for something.

I want to get as far as possible from Bristol, but I don't head in any particular direction. I ride slow, my headlight on, cold flakes of snow flicking into my eyes. Eventually I'll take Beer Can's advice and get some sunglasses or goggles. For now I just squint and lean into it.

Riding in the snow is a fitting punishment.

Wind beats at my cheeks, icy fingers tugging back my skin. I push the bike harder when I get to the freshly plowed and sanded 69. Sand, I know, is a motorcyclist's archenemy, but I don't care. Gloved fingers tighten on the handlebars. If I go, at least I'll go feeling free.

Because lately I feel anything but.

Except when I'm with Olivia.

I follow 69 back down through Wolcott, dodging traffic. Connecticut drivers should know how to drive in the fucking snow, but they don't. I weave between cars and give the finger to the ones who honk.

Cutting over Manor Avenue, I turn onto Meriden Road. It's only then that I realize I knew exactly where I was going.

Even with the snow, Pine Grove Cemetery looks the same as it did when I last saw it. A childhood friend of mine is buried here, but so is someone else. I slow to a near crawl as I enter the cemetery, scanning graves. I wasn't allowed to attend the funeral, so I don't know where they buried him. Not that I would've gone, anyway. Maybe to spit on his grave.

I'm not really sure why I'm here.

I head to Devon McKennan's grave, bowing my head and staring at the little plate that marks his resting place. I'm not a religious man. I don't believe in any god or higher power. But I do think that the people we love look out for us from the other side. Unfortunately for me, Devon and I weren't close enough for that kind of favor. I still felt the hole he left behind when he died, though.

I press two fingers to my lips, then touch them to the small headstone.

The cemetery is desolate in the winter, even more so underneath the falling snow. I leave my motorcycle parked near Devon and wander the rows of resting souls. I know he's here somewhere.

As time passes, my toes grow cold and then numb in my boots. The hoodie and vest do little to keep me warm with the rapidly falling temperature, but the snow has slowed, which means I'll get home in one piece. On the other side of the cemetery, I give up. I'm not going to find him. It's just as well, because I don't really have a good reason to visit.

"Fuck it," I mutter. Turning, I start back toward Devon. My gaze snags on a fairly newer looking headstone—less dark than some of the others. Even though it's two decades old, it's held up nicely. I guess my aunt and uncle splurged. My skin crawls at the thought, my balls drawing up into themselves. Blood pounds through my veins.

Lucy may have forgiven them, but I never will.

The engraving reads SEBASTIAN DEMMEL, BELOVED BROTHER, FATHER, UNCLE. My blood boils. If I thought I could actually knock it down, I'd kick the fucking thing. Instead, I step forward.

I tower over it, staring at the photo set under glass or plastic—whatever the fuck it is. His bald head gleams, those dead eyes looking directly into the camera. Guess they couldn't find a better picture.

"Hello, Sebastian," I growl in a low voice, even though there's no one around. Only the dead. "Looks like I'm still standing while you're on the floor." I smirk. "Or six feet under."

There should be some grand revelation here for me, like maybe I'll suddenly be able to let go of all this anger inside of me. But none of that died the day I killed him. If anything, it only backdrafted, igniting every inch of me. I burn like an underground coal mine.

"I'm going to take your fucking club," I tell him, nodding. "That's right. I'm gonna be President. You'll see, Bastard." His old nickname. I don't even really want to hold office, but it seems poetic enough. After all, I'm technically the prince—heir to the biker throne.

I'm just grateful that my father's reign didn't last long enough to destroy it.

Straightening the cut, I leer down at the grave. "I'd kill you again. Over and over." I turn and walk away.

The last grave that I visit is on an opposite end. Her final wishes insisted that she not be buried near him. Devon's, my father's, and my mother's graves all make a triangle, maybe even the kind that will suck me in and hold me prisoner. I find her easily enough. I always have.

I dust off snow from the small rectangle that marks her. She didn't really have family, so there wasn't anyone to splurge. There's barely enough room for her engraving: RUTH WOOD, MOTHER. Now that I'm out and working, I'm going to change that.

"Hey, Mom," I say gently, tracing the letters with a finger.

Where thinking of my father turns my blood to lava, the thought of my mother dissolves me, returning me to the little boy who found her in the tub. Her hands were still warm. The investigation was open and closed immediately after, because the coroner found a high dose of fentanyl and Ambien in her blood. Technically she passed out before she drowned. But my father was too cavalier about the whole thing, and I've always wondered.

"Sorry it took me so long to get here." I pause, taking a long, deep breath in through my nose. The guilt is suffocating. I should have come sooner. "You should see Lucy," I say, because I can't think of what else to tell her. My mom always adored my cousin. If she'd been around, I think she would've been the one to kill my father.

"And," I continue, the corners of my mouth twitching into a smile, "you should meet her sister. Well, sort of. She's adopted." I click my jaw back and forth. "She's great, Mom," I saw softly. "You'd like her."

And she would. She'd also be able to give me some pointers. My mom may've had me young, but she had a lot of class. She took the shit everyone gave her with a blissful grace, letting their comments roll right off her. Which is why I can't imagine her purposing overdosing on painkillers and sleeping pills, then stepping into a bathtub. She'd never so much as spent a day in bed, never mind slipping into a suicidal depression.

It just doesn't add up.

Sometimes I miss her terribly, especially now that I'm out. Not only was she my mom, but she was also a mother to Lucy, whose own parents lived in a coke-induced bubble. Still do. I'm honestly surprised that DCF let them adopt a little girl—especially after what they let happen to Lucy.

My blood is simmering again, so it's time to go.

"See ya later, Mom," I whisper, leaving her a kiss. The stone plate is ice beneath the pads of my fingers. I try not to think of her, trapped in a box in that cold ground.

I jump back on the Screamin' Eagle and head home to Lucy's. Today has been all over the fucking place. It was probably a bad idea to go to the cemetery, but sooner or later I would've had to.

I'm nearly home when my phone buzzes in my pocket. Pulling over, I press it to my ear.

"Prospect," Beer Can grunts, "we need you here at the club house."

I frown, blinking snowflakes off my eyelashes. "What's going on?" I was really looking forward to warming up in the living room with a hot cup of coffee.

"Club business." Beer Can sounds exasperated. "You don't need to know the whats and the whys. I say jump, you hop onto that club property that we were so kind to give you, and you just get your fucking ass here."

Someone's in a mood. "Yes sir," I intone. I hang up, tucking the phone back into my pocket. For several seconds, I stare up into the gray void of the sky. I need a break before I step back into the fray, but apparently I'm not going to get it. Letting my shoulders drop, I roll my neck back and forth. I probably look strange as fuck, standing on the shoulder of the road, my bike between my legs, staring up at the sky. But I have a feeling that it's the last moment of peace I'm going to get.

14

The sunlight slanting in through the front windows of the veterinarian's waiting room does little to calm me as I pace the small area. Somehow, Dio survived the night. They were able to set his tiny bones and, after several imaging tests, determined that no damage was done to his internal organs. At least, none that won't heal in time.

I just want to see him. The assistant already warned me that he's heavily sedated so that he can get better, but I don't care.

I didn't sleep last night, and not because I was scared that Eli would come back. No tiny bell tinkled intermittently, letting me know Dio was prowling the apartment. It felt strange not having him there.

My phone vibrates in my bag. I tug it free and read the text from Esther: "We found tires. Waiting for the guys to put them on. Be back ASAP."

But my shoulders only sag with partial relief. Esther was cool enough to let my rent slide for the month, that way I could afford both Dio's care *and* the tires. But between that and stopping at Walmart last night to buy a new lock set for the apartment, I'm officially tapped.

Then there's school to think about.

I resume pacing. I should be at my internship right now. For the most part, it isn't really a big deal. I'm already behind. But eventually I have to return to campus, and I still haven't figured out how I'm going to handle this.

The gun is a comforting weight in my purse, but it's not like I can shoot Eli in the face in broad daylight. Nor will he try anything during the day, surrounded by hundreds of people on campus. Besides, as far as he's concerned, right now I have no idea who's stalking me. He's still the nice guy from my photography class who let me borrow a camera and hangs out with me at lunch.

Which doesn't make any of this any less disturbing.

Nibbling on my lip, I begin my circuit of the tiny room again. Somehow I have to lure Eli out to a secluded place where no one will interrupt him. But it has to be somewhere I have the advantage. Having a gun doesn't necessarily mean I'll be the one to walk away. He's still bigger than me, and he's already proven that he's smart.

I still have no idea how he got into my apartment.

The thought sends chills down my spine. Maybe I *am* a little scared. I guess it'd be weird if I wasn't. My mind flashes to Dio, mangled and bloody in my bed. A sob escapes my lips.

Nope, not scared.

Pissed.

A door opens and the assistant pokes her head out. "Come on in, Mom," she says, her voice warm.

I pick up Dio's carrier and follow her into the small exam room.

My kitten lays on the stainless steel table in a bundle of towels. Someone's dressed him in a preemie-sized onesie covered in tiny ducks. Sensing my presence, Dio cracks an eye open and makes a small monkey squeak.

Tears sting my eyes. I cross the room and rub his little nose.

His eyes close peacefully, body rising and falling in steady rhythm.

I face the assistant. "He's going to be okay?"

She nods, launching into an explanation of exactly what they did and the medications he'll have to take. I'm delighted to be sticking my fingers into his mouth and force-feeding him pills— bites be damned. Since he's still so young and has such a strong spirit, she tells me, he should heal pretty well. But I shouldn't be alarmed if he walks with a limp, and she thinks that his tail will be permanently crooked.

My hands clench into fists, eyes narrowing to dam a fresh well of tears.

"Ms. Reynolds," the assistant says gently, gesturing for me to sit, "I really think we should fill out a police report. This is animal cruelty, and punishable by law—"

I scoff, cutting her off. "Do you really think the cops are going to run around chasing a cat beater?" My voice breaks.

She takes a deep breath. "It's not just Dio's safety at risk." Her eyes probe mine. "Right?"

"I changed my locks." I stand. "Can I take him home now?"

"Of course," she says. She helps me put him in the carrier, which has a removable top. I've padded the hell out of the thing with T-shirts, towels, and blankets. My little prince should have a relatively smooth ride home.

The veterinary assistant runs me through his meds one more time, then reminds me of his followup appointment for the removal of his stitches. "And if you change your mind about the police report," she says, handing me a business card, "I can back you up." Then she returns to her work.

I text Esther, but she's still waiting on her car. I'm dying for a cigarette, but I don't want to take Dio outside. It's too cold. So I resume pacing, leaving him on a chair where I can see him. I'm not letting him out of my sight—at least not for the time being.

Eventually I'll have to leave his side again. I have to be okay with that. Life has to go on. My locks are changed and there was no sign of forced entry, so we should all be safe now.

Nibbling my lip, I think of Esther's tires. There's nothing stopping Eli from slashing them again. But, I remind myself as I pass the front windows, he initially thought they were mine. Esther isn't his target.

It's me that he wants.

My phone buzzes. "Donny's coming to get you guys," Esther's text reads.

I glance out the window. I don't want to be alone with Donny. Not because I'm afraid of him. Despite his wide shoulders and corded muscles, the dude's a teddy bear. Esther wouldn't be with him if he was an asshole. But as soon as we're alone, he's going to push for me to tell Cliff. I already know it. Maybe I'm being stubborn, but I've been taking care of myself my whole life. I don't need Prince Charming to ride in on his motorcycle and shoot down my dragon. I've got my own gun. I'll slay my own monsters.

Donny pulls up and jumps out, leaving the engine idling. He strides into the clinic, glancing around. His eyes land on me, then flick to Dio in his carrier.

"Oh, thank God," he says. Crossing the room, he engulfs me in a bear hug.

I stiffen, but only because neither Donny nor any of the other guys have ever hugged me. It's a bit awkward. His embrace is warm, though, and his cologne smells just as pleasant as it feels to be in his arms. I relax against him. It's a purely platonic hug. Even if he wasn't with Esther, Donny is old enough to be my father.

Not that age ever stopped me from fucking Cliff's brains out.

Still, there's just something benevolent and protective about Donny that makes me trust him. It's a gut feeling, and my gut is never wrong. Which is precisely why I want him to keep his mouth shut. It's bad enough I have one River Reaper hovering around me like a nervous mother. I don't know Cliff very well, but

I've spent enough time with him to know what he'd do to Eli if I told him. Especially since I know he was away for twenty years.

You don't do hard time on small offenses like assault.

Donny steps away, blinking away moisture in his eyes. "Looking at that little guy last night," he says, moving over to Dio's carrier, "I didn't think he was gonna make it." He peers in through the small holes cutout in the sides. "He's sleeping. He looks good."

"He does," I agree, joining him. I lift the carrier as gently as possible, trying not to rock Dio around too much. Donny holds the door for me and we head out.

I'm not sure whether it's my imagination or not, but Donny is driving more carefully than usual, avoiding potholes and bumps, and actually obeying the 25 mph speed limit. He follows Wolcott Street, then takes a very gentle left onto Lakewood.

"We got a good deal on tires." He slows as we near McDonald's. "You hungry? I told Essie I'd grab something on our way back."

I smile at the nickname. It's too fucking cute. Give it a few months, and these two will be planning their wedding. I wonder if Esther knows what she's getting herself into. Donny may be a good guy, but he's still the club Enforcer. I don't know exactly what kind of business he handles, but it sure as hell isn't kitten sitting.

Donny pulls into the drive-thru and orders enough food for an army. I sneak a fry out of the large bag sitting between us.

"Between you and Cliff, I'm gonna get fat." I shake my head in disapproval.

"Red Dog? Oh yeah. Dude *loves* his Mickey D's."

I frown. "Red Dog?" My maybe-boyfriend has a weird ass nickname and I'm the last to know about it.

"Yeah," Donny rasps, "from his time in the pen. It started off as a joke, but from what I'm hearing, it kinda morphed after he busted a few noses. He was always walking around covered in other people's blood."

Lifting an eyebrow, I stare at Donny. "How do you know this?"

His big shoulders rise and fall. "Aw, sweetheart." He drives past the tire shop, heading toward the top of the hill.

"Where are we going?" My pulse thrums in my veins. The hairs on my arms and the back of my neck stand up.

Donny casts sidelong glances at me in between peeks at the road. Though it's stopped snowing, the pavement is still slick in some places. "I've gotta look you in the eyes while I tell you this, darlin'."

"Tell me what?" Now I'm on high alert. I wrap my arms around Dio's carrier, trying to decide whether I should push open the door and bail, or if I should wait 'til we get to wherever we're going. It seems pretty ironic that I might have to pull my gun on the guy who gave it to me.

He pulls into the parking lot of an abandoned restaurant. The tires roll over the untouched snow. Donny tucks us far enough away from the road that we won't be bothered, but turns around so that we're facing the parking lot exit.

"You're freaking me out, Donny." I slug down ice cold Dr. Pepper in a feeble attempt to cool my burning nerves.

"I'm sorry, kiddo." He puts the truck in park and turns in his seat. His eyes lock with mine. "We took a vote."

I wait, as still as a deer.

"Ravage and I wanted to tell you years ago, but you know how it goes. We finally got all the guys to agree." Opening the bag of food, he plucks a fry from a cardboard container.

I roll my eyes, partially in relief but also because he's taking forever to spit out whatever it is. I grab a couple more fries, more to keep myself busy.

"See, I can't talk to you in front of Essie because I asked her and she told me she doesn't want to have anything to do with club business. But Olivia . . ." Golden brown eyes search mine, almost pleadingly. "You've always been a part of the family."

"Gee, thanks, Donny," I say, "but you've only known me for like a year."

He grimaces. "Yeah . . . no. That's not true. I've known you since you were a baby."

My eyebrows furrow. I'm not sure how what he's saying can be possible. My parents are completely unaffiliated with the club— both them and my biological parents. As far as I know, anyway. My eyes widen, the pieces falling into place. "No," I whisper. Not because I'm denying it, but because it seems impossible.

Donny nods. "Yes, babygirl. Your daddy—your *real* father—is Mercy Reynolds. He's one of the founders of the River Reapers. He and Bastard Demmel built this club."

"Demmel?" I parrot.

"Red Dog's father." Donny's lips flatten. "Ya'll have some serious family history to discuss."

Rubbing my temples, I pat around for the door handle. The air in the truck is suddenly too heavy. I shove the door open, then maneuver Dio's carrier around in my lap until he's on the passenger seat and I'm slipping out. I close the door and walk away several paces, lighting up as soon as I'm a safe distance away. My kitten doesn't need secondhand smoke on top of broken bones, bruises, and lacerations.

I turn around, not surprised to see Donny joining me. I hold out my pack to him, but he shakes his head.

"Anything else I should know about?" I feel like my world's been tilted on its axis. Up until two minutes ago, I had no idea who my birth father was. All I know is that my birth mother had been fourteen when she got pregnant. She raised me until I was eight. I remember every detail of the day the police came to our apartment and took me away, but I don't talk about it. There was never any reason to. Lucy's parents—*my* parents—have been nothing but good to me, if not a little heavy on the partying.

"Olivia, your daddy's still alive," Donny says quietly.

My hand stops halfway to my lips. The cigarette burns in front of me. "What?"

"Reason why we know so much about Red Dog is because he was inside with Mercy. One of us visits every so often, catches him up. And he filled us in on Red Dog." Donny touches my arm. "You're pale, girl."

Hand shaking, I bring the cigarette to my lips. "So you're telling me," I say in a steady but dead voice, "that I was able to see him, and had no fucking idea?" I think of the week we spent in Lewisburg. I have a father. An alive father. Who is mine. And I could have visited, but instead hopped right back on the train, completely oblivious.

Donny nods. He lets me process this for a few beats. Then, very quietly, he says, "There's more."

"Jesus fucking Christ." I throw up my hands. "Is this why you bought me McDonald's? To soften the blow?" I shake my head. "I don't want to know."

"You do, though." Donny gently takes my shoulders. "Olivia, you *do*."

I can't believe any of this. For one, why the fuck didn't Lucy's parents tell me? And why did I go into foster care if I had a breathing relative? Too many questions swirl through my head, and I'm not sure I want the answers. My father is a River Reaper. That blood runs through me. The club is just as much a part of me as it is Cliff.

"Wait," I say. "Is this why I got the job? Not because of my certification or ability to mix good drinks. But because of the fucking club?"

Donny winces. "We took a vote," he says.

"Fuck your vote." I hurl the words at him. "None of you thought maybe you might wanna get me up to speed?"

"Big things like that have to be unanimous," he explains. "But your job was undisputed. The vote was more of a formality. We promised your dad that we'd take care of you."

"Oh, enough of that bullshit." My cigarette is down to the filter. I flick it into the snow and light another. "I don't need your charity. I'll start looking for something else." Or maybe, I muse, I'll move down to Lewisburg and take something there. Someone's going to have to be around when my father gets out—and it sure as fuck can't be this good for nothing club. "A vote," I mutter, shaking my head.

"That would kill Ravage," Donny says. "And your dad." He lifts my chin with a gentle finger. "Don't you get it, darlin'? You're with us so we can watch out for you. Your daddy didn't want you all alone while he's behind bars." Turning his head, he spits into the snow. "Your goddamn mother—"

I jerk away and hold up my hands. "Enough. I'm done." Turning, I stalk back toward the pickup. I can't deal with any more of this conversation, with anything else he has to tell me. I need Lucy. She's older than me, but she would've told me if she already knew. I wonder if our parents know.

I pull myself up into the truck, careful not to jar Dio. When Donny gets in, I tell him to take me to Lucy's. He doesn't argue. "Just tell Esther I had some shit to take care of," I mutter. My entire body feels like it's been sucked dry, every ounce of life depleted from the very marrow of my bones.

Even though I know it's not Donny's fault, I still hold it against him. During the entire ride to Lucy's, I keep my mouth shut. He doesn't deserve my company. I don't even thank him for the food. When we pull up to my sister's condo, I grab several containers of fries and wrapped burgers, stuffing them into my purse.

The heaviest of conversations couldn't kill my appetite.

I nod goodbye to Donny, then climb out, taking Dio with me. He lets out a mew that's more a sigh than anything else.

"It's okay, baby," I soothe. "We're just making a pit stop."

Donny waits until I get inside the door, earning back some points in my book. Closing it behind me, I put down Dio's carrier.

The familiar calm of my sister's home envelopes me. Then I remember.

Lucy's at work.

Before I can check out the front window, strong arms grab me from behind.

15

CLIFF

Olivia kicks against me, the ball of her foot smashing against my shin. I release her, and hold my hands up, palms out. She whips around, fists up. They drop when recognition dawns on her face.

"You did work," I say, grinning through a wince.

She sags against the closed front door, though, face pale. She sinks to the carpet and draws her knees to her chest.

"Liv?" I cross the distance between us and sit next to her.

Blinking away tears, she shakes her head over and over again. It's a steady hand that brushes her hair out of her eyes, though, and I know my girl's going to be okay. Still, I wrap an around around her and pull her close.

"Sorry I scared you," I whisper into her hair.

Her head snaps up, though, as if she's already showed too much vulnerability for too long. Those eyes ice over—a look I'm more than familiar with. Olivia is trapped in her own prison.

She lifts her chin. "What do you know about Mercer Reynolds?" A cold, calculating gaze searches my face.

"The name doesn't really ring a bell," I say, "but isn't that your last name?"

"Mercy, then?" Her face is as hard as white marble, the usual contours of her cheeks gone.

I shrug. "Olivia, what's this about?" I hug her closer, even though her body is rigid.

"You should know." Her voice is sharp and accusing. "You were in prison with him!" Those eyes glare up at me.

Frowning, I churn the name around in my head. During my sentence, I mostly kept to myself. I didn't need the usual color-coded protection because I'd killed a child molester. In even the hardest criminals' eyes, I was a hero—which meant I avoided the others. For the most part, they avoided me too.

I close my eyes and go back in time, floating through concrete halls and a blur of faces. Mercy. The name does sound familiar.

Then I remember.

"He came in after me," I tell her, eyes still closed. "He banded up with the whites. Not the Nazis. There were a few white groups." I remember seeing him a few times in the courtyard. He was in max, so we didn't cross paths often. He wasn't any taller than anyone else, but he had a presence about him. Jet black hair. And those same goddamn eyes.

My own eyes open, zeroing in on Olivia's immediately. "I can't believe I didn't see it," I mutter.

"So it's true?" Her eyes fill up with tears, and I can't tell whether she's furious or what. "Mercy is alive?"

"You want to catch me up here?" I nod for her to follow me to my room. Even though Lucy has a strict no smoking policy, it's cold as fuck outside. And I picked up this cigarette smell neutralizing spray shit the other day. It smells like crisp mountains or something equally fake.

I've officially been domesticated.

We sit on my bed, my back against the wall and Olivia in my arms. My legs form protective walls around her. Smoke curls into the air for several long minutes.

Then she tells me what Donny told her.

"Did you ever talk to him?" she asks, twisting around to meet my eyes.

"A few times." I glance down at my cigarette, mind spinning. Yet another way that we're connected. And here we sit, on my bed —the rightful heirs to the club. I suck in a deep breath. "Olivia, there's something you need to know. About me." And us, but I don't say so.

She closes her eyes, a long blink. "I just want to know what he's like. Who he is."

"And I'll tell you," I promise. "But first you need to know who *my* father is."

She turns in my arms until she's facing me. Drawing her limbs into a cross-legged position, she sits with her knees touching mine. "Shoot," she says.

"Sebastian Demmel," I say, nearly choking on his name in disgust. "Or Bastard." I pause, feeling bile rising up in my throat. This is more Lucy's story than mine. It almost feels like a violation of her privacy. But if we're going to be caught in this web, then Olivia needs to know the truth.

All of it.

"Lucy's parents—*your* parents—worked a lot of the same shifts, so she was always over at my house. I loved her, Livvie. We were both only-children, and there weren't any other cousins in the family yet." I smile as memories of chasing Lucy around my backyard skip through my head. I take a deep breath.

"She used to stay overnight." Grimacing, I shake my head. "I can't give you the details, but she started having nightmares. She was so confused. She'd beg her parents to let her stay home, but she still always wanted to see me." I light another cigarette, hands shaking. "Finally, she told her parents."

I look Olivia straight in the eye, pain pulsing in my temples. "Sebastian," I spit out his name, "was . . . hurting her." The familiar searing ripping in my chest splits my heart. My fingers twitch in reflex. I bring the cigarette to my lips, pulling in a long drag until my lungs burn.

"Jesus," Olivia whispers, wrapping her arms around herself. "He was molesting her?"

I nod, my jaw flexing. The fire rips through me. I'm standing in that kitchen all over again. "I'd been out at work. No one else believed her. I didn't know she was coming over that night. When I got home—" My voice breaks. I turn away, staring ruefully at the wall. I don't want to repeat what I saw before the red washed it away.

I suck in a deep breath. "I pushed him away from her and shoved her aside. I think she hit her head on the cabinet doors. But she curled up and backed into the corner. Then I lifted him off the chair." I shake my head. "He was so much bigger than me, but somehow I did it. And—" My lips curl into a vengeful smile.

In the dying light of the bedroom, I must look like a jack-o-lantern.

Olivia says nothing, though. She just watches me, listening, her chest barely rising and falling.

"I threw him onto the floor. My fists kept pounding into his face." I can still hear the way they sounded, flesh connecting with raw meat. A sort of heavy, wet smacking. "Broke his nose, caved in a cheekbone. And I kept hitting him."

I look down at my hands, the cigarette limp between two fingers. "Then I wrapped my hands around his neck. And put all of my weight into it." I blink, remembering how his legs kicked out, arms jerking. "There was still some fight in him. I snuffed it out."

I look at Olivia again. "I killed my own father, Olivia."

"You saved Lucy," she begins, but I cut her off.

"I enjoyed every second of it," I say. "I didn't do it to help Lucy. I did it because I wanted to, because I knew it would feel good." I lean forward. "And I would do it again."

"It felt good," she echoes.

"Yes." I stub out my cigarette. "This is what I am, Olivia. This is why you need to stay away from me. Because I snap. I lose control, and the urge takes over." I think of all the men I beat up. The ones who preyed on the quiet men, the few that dared to fuck with me. The time in seg was always worth it.

"One of the few times I spoke to Mercy," I say, "he complimented me. He said, 'Nice form.' And then he walked away. He didn't even bother asking me to join his group. He knew I didn't need them."

I show her my hands. "I've *touched* you with these. How does that feel?"

She stares at me with wide eyes. No fear swims in them, though. Her nostrils flare. "Like I want you to touch me again," she whispers.

Then she's in my lap, hands grabbing my face and crushing my lips to hers. Those long legs wrap around my waist, and she pries my lips open. "Fuck me, Cliff," she breathes into my mouth.

And I want to—physically, anyway. Maybe even emotionally, whatever the fuck that means. But I can't. Because I've now shown her who I am. Now that she's seen a glimpse of the monster, there's no happy ending here. We're not going to make love and then fall asleep in each other's arms.

It ends now.

I push her out of my lap. Not hard enough to send her flying, but enough to get her attention. "No," I growl. I stand from the bed and pace the room.

Jumping up from the bed, she touches my arm with a delicate hand. "Cliff, you did what you had to—"

I shove her hand away. "Everyone keeps saying that." Caging her, I back her up against a wall. I press my body into hers. "Don't you get it?" I seethe. "You're playing with fire, little girl."

Her hands strain at my chest, her mouth twisted. "You're telling yourself the wrong story, Cliff." Those luminous eyes meet mine. They glint with lust—and something else. A fire that I can't name. It makes me want to claim her even more, to make her mine forever.

But I can't.

I lean in, our noses touching. "Become a social worker," I rasp. "Get out of this town, and save little kids. But don't ever come near me again."

Her eyes flicker. "Don't do this, Cliff." She isn't pleading. Her voice is hard. Like she's so much wiser than I am, like she can see the future.

I have to let her go, though.

Gripping her arms, I press her hard against the wall. Lucy will be home soon. And I have to leave.

I release her, resisting the urge to kiss those lips one last time. Then, grabbing my cut, I brush past her. As I walk through the living room, I hear a tiny meow. My gaze snags on the cat carrier on the floor, wondering why Olivia would bring Dio over to Lucy's. But it doesn't matter. I have to get moving, get out of here before Lucy gets home and talks me out of this.

I slam the front door behind me, and Olivia doesn't follow. Even as I stomp on the kick starter, I sort of hope that she will. But this isn't a fucking Disney movie, and my resolve has to be solid. For her safety, and for mine.

I let the Screamin' Eagle speak for me as I roar away, locking my heart down as tightly as the engine welded underneath me.

PULLING into the parking lot of The Wet Mermaid, I decide I really need a second vehicle. The roads were slippery, and I nearly wiped out a few times. I don't want to outdo Skid. He can keep that title.

I find Beer Can inside, sitting at the bar. Seeing it is a stinging reminder of Olivia. Of course, she isn't here. A woman I've never seen is currently serving, but that doesn't say much. I'm still an alien here.

"You're late," Beer Can says without looking at me.

I sit on the stool next to him. "Yeah. I got caught up in something." I shake my head at him. Since I'm a Prospect, I'm not included in Church or votes. I'm pretty much in the dark. But I'm seriously pissed that they sprung all of the Mercy shit on Olivia without giving me a heads up.

"Something you wanna say?" Beer Can eyes me, bloodshot and red-rimmed.

"No." It comes out a gruff rasp, harder than I intended. But fuck it. I'm in a shitty mood.

"Can I get you something, honey?" the bartender asks. Golden hair flows over her shoulders, cascading to her hips.

There isn't a drink in the world that is strong enough, but I order a whiskey on the rocks.

"Now that you've got your sippy cup," Beer Can says, standing, "follow me. I've got a job for you."

He leads me to the rooms upstairs, then knocks at a closed door. A woman's voice answers, and he pushes it open.

She sits on the bed, black chin-length hair tucked behind her ears. I peg her at about my age. The clothes she's wearing are a mix of a size too big and too small—a mashup of donations, from the looks of them. Bruises mar her face and neck. The clothes cover the rest of them. It's just a guess, but from the way she ducks her head, I'd say it's worse than that.

"Cliff, this is Bree." Beer Can nods to us both in introduction. "She's your job."

Holding my whiskey, I look back and forth between them.

"Bree is a friend of the club. She needs a ride to the train station." Beer Can tosses me a set of keys. "You're taking the blue Chevy."

I raise my eyebrows. "I don't have a license."

"That hasn't stopped you from riding that bike around," he remarks.

"Yes," I say slowly, "but we're talking about driving into New Haven. Lots of cops. Spot checks. Shit like that."

Beer Can laughs, crossing his arms. "Well, well, well." His eyes skewer me. "Don't ask questions. Just do what you're fucking told." He picks up a duffel bag from the floor and shoves it into my arms. "Take the lady to the train station, Prospect. When you get back, you can take her room."

He leaves us, swaying as he heads down the hall.

I turn to look at Bree. She stands from the bed, hugging herself.

"Well," she says, "shall we?"

I CHAINSMOKE AS I DRIVE, eyes flitting from the rearview mirror to the side mirrors to the windshield. This whole thing makes me nervous as fuck. Strange woman, unlicensed driver. Probably an unregistered car. Maybe they're testing me to see how loyal I am.

"So how do you tie in with the club?" I ask, stopping at one of Naugatuck's million stop signs. My plan is to avoid the highway and 63. It's going to take us forever to get to New Haven. At least I don't have dinner plans.

"Oh, well, you know." I glance at her. She smiles. "I help out here and there. They help me." Her shoulders lift and fall.

"That's not vague." I light another cigarette. "Are you a hooker?"

Bree snorts. "Are you a bank manager?"

My eyebrow twitches. I check the speedometer. I'm pushing the speed limit. Letting off the gas a little, I try to put the pieces together. Donny is the club's Enforcer. Beer Can is the Sergeant-At-Arms. Bree is a friend of the club who's wearing an awful lot of bruises. "Who are you running from?"

The laughter dies on her lips. "No one," she says. "Not anymore."

Bingo.

I relax back into the driver's seat. "Where are you going?"

"New Haven," she replies. "That's where you're taking me, isn't it?"

"Yeah, the train station." I glance at her again. She's staring out her window, probably looking for ghosts. "How far out of state do they want you to go?"

"My, my. There are some brains behind that handsome face." She shifts in her seat, and I notice the edge of a tattoo on her wrist. She pulls her sleeve down before I can get a good look at it.

"Sounds like this is a regular thing for you." I hold my pack of cigarettes out to her over the center console.

She pushes them back to me. "That's pretty presumptuous for someone who just met me fifteen minutes ago."

"Look, I'm not looking down on you." I rake hair back from my face. "I'm just wondering . . . Aren't you tired of running?" I know I am.

Bree doesn't answer.

After ten minutes, the silence starts to get to me. I turn on PLR, since I've recently discovered that WMRQ is no longer the alternative rock station that I grew up with. PLR mostly plays classic rock like Def Leppard and Tesla, but they slide in some Stone Temple Pilots and the like every so often.

The closer we get to New Haven, the more Bree checks the time on the dashboard. I don't know what time her train leaves, but it must be soon. Ditching the back roads for 63, I push the speedometer as far as I can without truly speeding. I just hope we don't hit the regular gridlock.

Whoever designed New Haven's network of one-way streets was an asshole with a sadistic sense of humor.

Traffic in the city isn't bad, but it's still slow. Bree fidgets in her seat, looking more and more like she's going to eject herself from the car and run the rest of the way. We inch toward Union Station. I'm not the one catching the train but I'm starting to feel anxious, too. If I fuck this up and Bree misses her train, I have a feeling I'll be losing more than my cut.

But traffic starts flowing again, and I pull in front of the station at 5:39.

Bree grabs her duffel bag from the backseat.

"Am I walking you in?" I don't remember whether Beer Can said.

But Bree shakes her head. "My train is for 5:45. I've got to haul ass." She leans over and gives me an almost motherly peck on the cheek. With one hand, she pushes open the passenger door. Then she climbs out, slamming the door shut behind her. She starts to walk away, then pauses. Turns.

I roll down the window. "Gonna give me a tip?"

A smile touches her eyes. "Take care of my daughter, Cliff."

Then she turns and disappears inside.

16

OLIVIA

By the time Lucy gets home from work, I've composed myself. I've even fixed my makeup and fed Dio some canned tuna. Watching him wolf it down soothes me in more ways than I can list. I sit at the table reading for one of my classes on my phone when she walks in.

Despite my efforts, though, she takes one look at me and clucks her tongue. "I'll kill him. What did he do?"

Big sisters always know.

I'm not even sure where to start. I look down at my hands. "Hope you don't mind that I brought a date." I nod to Dio, who's passed out in a heap of towels on the floor.

Lucy's face transforms from concerned sister to laser-shooting rage dragon. "Cliff did that?" She looks from me to Dio, appalled.

"*No*," I say, beckoning for her to sit down. I suck in a deep breath and steal a glance at my purse.

"Go ahead," Lucy says, rolling her eyes.

I light up, grateful, but consider busting Cliff for smoking in his room. Not that it matters. He isn't coming back.

I slump back in my seat.

"Out with it, kid," Lucy says. "I've had a long day. Six-year-olds are exhausting. It's like they can sense spring vacation coming up." She eyes my cigarettes, which is odd because I've never seen my sister smoke, or heard her mention it. And we tell each other everything.

I envision myself telling her all about Eli, how he initially seemed cute but worked his way up to creeping around my apartment and nearly killing my cat. But I can't tell her all of it, because then she'll never let me go home. And I can't even use Esther and Donny as a compromise, because my roommate texted me earlier to let me know that she and Donny are going away for the weekend.

They've been dating for less than a week, and they're already going away together. I hate to admit it to myself, but I desperately want that with Cliff.

Lucy whistles. "Okay, Olivia, come on out of the rabbit hole."

I sigh again. "Dio got out and a car hit him," I say, waving a nonchalant hand. My stomach twists with guilt. I should be telling Lucy all about how angry I am. Instead all I can think about is Cliff, just up and leaving me here because he's "too dangerous." My lip curls.

My sister stands and pulls a bottle of wine out from the refrigerator. "We're going to play a game," she says, grabbing two wine glasses from a cabinet. "And I really hope I don't lose, because I can't afford a hangover on top of first graders." She sets it all down on the table.

Pouring us each a glass, she announces the rules. "Every time I have to prompt you, you have to drink. And every time you give me details without me asking, I have to drink."

I arch an eyebrow at her. "That is the worst game you've made up. Ever."

She shrugs. "I told you I was tired." She clinks her glass to mine. "Let the games begin."

I stare at her. "Luce, you do realize that all we have to do is not talk and the whole thing collapses . . . right?"

"Fine." She takes a sip. "We just drink. And you talk. *Now*."

It takes me two gulped down glasses before I'm lubricated enough to spill everything that's happened today. I'm sober enough that I can easily leave out everything about Eli. I tell her what Donny told me about my father, and she refills both of our glasses without asking.

Then, without meeting her eyes, I tell her about my conversation with Cliff.

"He told me what happened," I say slowly. "Why he went to prison." I sip wine to continue avoiding looking at her.

Out of the corner of my eye, though, I see her mouth make a tiny O. Her chest rises as she chooses her next words.

"You don't have to talk about it," I say quickly. "I guess he was trying to reciprocate. Or push me away. Or something." I polish off my third glass. I'm now comfortably buzzed, enough so that the words start flowing and tears prick at my eyes. "Fuck." I dab at them with the corner of my sleeve. "I *just* fixed my makeup."

"Livvie," Lucy says, her voice full of sisterly sympathy. She pushes a box of tissues toward me. This girl is so together, she has tissues in every room. And she never runs out of things like toilet paper or milk.

It's almost hard to believe that someone could hurt her the way that Cliff's father did.

My eyebrows scrunch together. I fucked the direct spawn of the man who molested my sister. In a way, that's seriously fucked up. Or maybe that's the wine talking. My frown deepens.

"Liv," Lucy says gently.

I look up, meeting her gaze.

"Cliff is . . . kind of like a twenty-year-old kid. He has no idea what he wants. He's just figuring everything out for himself." She blinks several times, and I realize my sister is on the verge of tears. "He's missed the most important years of his life," she whispers. "He's, like, emotionally stunted—and it's all my fault."

I grab her hand, squeezing. "*No*. It's not your fault! Cliff made that choice himself."

"He did it for me!" Her voice breaks. Tears rolls down her cheeks.

It kind of freaks me out. I don't think I've ever seen Lucy cry. I push the tissues back her way. "He's still the one who did it. I'm sure he knew what the consequences would be." I glower. He sure as hell better know what the consequences are now. I am never, ever letting him back in. "Asshole," I mutter.

Lucy dries her tears. "So what happened?" she says, voice thick with emotion.

I know she's just trying to deflect the conversation away from her, but I'm drunk and too clumsy to bat it back at her. "He went on about how he's so *dangerous* and blah, blah, blah." I roll my eyes, my voice too loud. "Basically, the whole 'you're too good for me' spiel."

"Pathetic." She crosses her arms. "Well, his loss."

My pursed lips twitch to the side.

"What?" Lucy peers at me. "It *is* his loss, Olivia."

"Then why," I draw out the word, "does it feel like mine?" I huff. This is all too weird. I'm not used to men turning my world upside down and inside out. I feel like someone's slit my body open and rearranged all of my organs. It's not a nice feeling, and it has nothing to do with the wine.

"You've got to focus on you, Livvie," my sister says in her preachy *I know better because I'm so much older* voice. "You have so much to offer in a relationship. Anyone who doesn't see that is . . . is . . ."

"Even if he's your childhood hero?" I scowl, eyeing the bottle of wine. There's enough left for one glass.

"Go for it." She pushes it toward me. "Look, Cliff may be like a brother to me, but *you* are my sister. Hos before bros, yo."

Cringing, I pour my glass. "Please don't ever say that again."

She shrugs. "But it's true. And you do have a lot to give—to someone who's really going to appreciate it."

"A lot to give? Luce, I've missed like seventy-five percent of my classes this week. I'm behind on my internship hours." I lift my voice into a southern twang. "My daddy's in prison." I giggle. "I'm a fucking country song."

"Too bad college radio stations don't usually play country," she jokes.

"Maybe they do down south." I tilt my head, pretending to contemplate. "I could move to Georgia or something, redo the semester..."

"You're a sneeze away from graduating." Lucy stands and puts her hands on her hips. "Don't you dare throw it all away over some guy."

If only she knew.

I rest my chin in the palm of my hand. "I wish I could go back in time." Add/drop that damn photography class. Or just never accept the camera from Eli. And definitely, for sure, not have sex with Cliff in someone's station wagon. I fold my arms on the table and bury my face in my sweater.

"Let me drive you home," Lucy says, rubbing my back. "It'll all look better in the morning. I promise."

I snort. "Like you're even sober enough to drive." My voice is muffled against the table.

"Pfft. How do you think I get through my week with these kids?"

Sitting up fast, I twist around to see her face. A smirk dances across her lips. "Luce, that's like borderline alcoholism."

She rolls her eyes. "I don't drink to function, Livvie. I have one or two glasses every night, after dinner and while I correct papers. It's my way of celebrating surviving another day in educational hell." She sighs. "I thought this teaching gig was going to be so different, you know?"

"You," I say, poking her in the ribs, "are ruining your own 'graduate in time' lecture."

She smooths my hair. "You're going to find that the world doesn't always meet your expectations. And that feeling, my friend, is called disillusionment. Learn to love wine." She pats my back. "Now come on. I've got to get up early, and I'm sure your kitty wants his territory back."

We both look over at Dio, who is happily munching away at the remainder of his tuna dinner.

"Are you sure about that?"

Lucy nods to my glass. "Chug it, woman."

Feeling pleasantly woozy, I obey. While I'm sucking down pink moscato, I decide that I'm going to continue this warm party when I get home. I'll draw a nice hot bath and bring a battered copy of one of my Terry Brooks novels with me. Maybe *The Elfstones of Shannara*, because I could really use a little Eretria in my life right now. Reading isn't really my jam, but I have nice memories of my mom—my birth mother—reading to me when I was little. The Shannara books are all I have left of her.

For all I know, she's dead, and I'm usually okay with that. I have my parents, and Lucy. My sister, especially, is always a comfort.

Except when she's practically dragging my drunk ass out the door.

I juggle Dio's carrier and my purse, casting a longing glance up the stairs where I know Cliff's room waits, empty.

"I'll text you if he comes home," Lucy promises. "Now *out*."

Lucy drops me off in front of my apartment with another bottle of wine and a kiss on the cheek.

"Take care of that kitty," she orders, "but take care of *you*, too."

In true Lucy fashion, she waits outside until I get in and lock up. I wave to her out the front window and she drives off. Sighing, I kick off my boots, then release Dio from his prison. He waddles over to his kitty bed and promptly crashes.

"That's looking like a fantastic idea," I say.

Fuck the bath, I decide. And, even though another glass of wine sounds heavenly, I really should get up early and actually go to class. Talk to my department head and professors, see what I can do about my internship.

Because Lucy is right. It isn't too late. I still have time to turn things around. I can still walk across that stage in May.

I tuck the bottle of wine into the refrigerator, knowing that Esther and I will totally make use of it when she gets back. Then I pad into my bedroom for the night, turning off lights as I make my way through the apartment. The only lights I leave on are the porch light and the lamp in the living room. Mostly because I feel bad about leaving Dio in the dark, even though he has night vision.

I undress in the black of my bedroom, trying not to think about what I found the last time I came home to an empty house. But Dio is safe. The locks are changed. My sheets have been thrown out and replaced.

Everything is fine.

Still, I flick on my light, because apparently my pleasant wine drunk has morphed into an all out paranoia. But my room is completely normal. It's exactly the way I left it. Even the array of makeup across my vanity is the same. It looks like Esther didn't dip into my stash before she left.

Everything is fine.

Except.

I gasp out loud, skittering back from the vanity as if it's going to reach out and grab for me. I crash into my bed, grunting in pain as my hip smacks into the wooden frame. Shaking it off, I glance around my room, looking for anything else out of place. Human hearts, maybe. But even the closet door is wide open, the way I left it. A signal of safety.

Still.

The shiny set of keys amidst my makeup glints in the light. I already know which locks they fit into.

Chest rising and falling in rapid breaths, I swallow hard. Glance around for my purse. It's by the bedroom door, where I dumped it. I cross the room and yank the gun out, screwing in the silencer.

Both my breath and pulse are loud in my ears. I open the door and peek out into the rest of the apartment. Dio's bell jingles, and I lurch, running in the direction of the sound, gun pointed.

But my kitten is just drinking water from his bowl.

I suck in a deep breath. "Get ahold of yourself, Olivia." Exhaling, I try to be logical. Maybe Esther left her keys because she's moving in with Donny and didn't have time to tell me.

My logical explanation has a major flaw: that's not like Esther at all.

I turn in a slow circle in the kitchen, taking stock. Fear pumps through me, sending pulses of adrenaline into my veins. But I don't know how to use it. I take another deep breath. The kitchen is in the same exact condition that I left it in.

Maybe I'm just losing it. Esther probably made an extra copy of our keys and left them for me. She was the one to go to Walmart for the copies, after all.

My shoulders sag. I lower the gun. As the adrenaline ebbs, I feel ridiculous. Still, I check the entire apartment. Room by room, I make sure windows are locked. I sweep Esther's bedroom, then close the door behind her. Then I double check the front door.

Locked.

Feeling a bit paranoid, I head to my bedroom. I pass by Dio sleeping on his back, his tummy rising and falling with each breath.

"Goodnight," I whisper, and slip into my room.

I change into a Mindless Self Indulgence T-shirt and peel back the covers on my bed. Another set of shiny keys rests on my pillow. This time, I flat out scream.

Turning, I snatch the gun from my vanity. Tears prick at my eyes. I gasp for breath, feeling as if my chest is being squeezed. Chills dot my body. Still sucking in sharp breaths, I turn back to the bed.

They're still there.

A whimper escapes my lips. He's fucking with me. Probably watching through my window right now and laughing at me. Except my blinds are down, the way I usually keep them. I stare at the window, wondering: If I pull them up or peek through, will I find him standing out in the yard?

"Think, Olivia," I whisper to myself. I can't let him scare me. If I get hysterical, he wins. I need to flip this around on him. Take back the higher ground.

But I can barely think with my heart pounding in my ears.

My phone vibrates in my bag. I dart across my bedroom and grab it. I don't recognize the number on the screen. It must be Eli. My thumb slides toward the green button to answer it, but I halt.

I can't play his game. If I answer it, he'll just keep playing with me.

I put the phone down on my bed. Then, leaving the light on and the door cracked open, I ease out of my room.

On the balls of my feet, I prowl the apartment. I tuck sleepy Dio into his carrier and close him in Esther's room. The whole time, I hear my phone vibrating in my bedroom.

Shrouded in shadows, I park myself in a corner of the living room. I drop to a crouch, gun drawn. If he comes in—no, *when* he comes in—he won't make it far.

I swallow hard, muscles coiled. My arms aren't used to being straight out for long, and after only a couple of minutes, they start to fall asleep. I flex my elbows, getting the blood pumping again. But my eyes never leave the door.

In my bedroom, my phone stops ringing.

Every beat of my heart is a hollow echo in my ears. Tears sting my eyes, whether from fatigue or fear, I don't know. I turn off the safety.

The door knob jiggles, the distinct sound of a key fitting into the lock cutting across the room to me. Even after seeing the spare keys he left for me, hearing it sends shockwaves of nausea through me.

He made copies of my apartment keys.

I picture him sitting in a dim cellar with an old fashioned key-making machine. My parents had one that was my great-grandfather's. All he had to do was take the blank to my apartment, notch it in the lock, and voila. Chills ripple up and down my spine.

I've put too much trust into this world, even after all I've seen. Safety is only an illusion. One that I've gladly wrapped myself in.

Until now.

Time slows, and I take a long, deep breath in through my nose. As the bottom lock disengages, I form a fast plan.

I'm not an experienced shooter. I won't be able to hit him while he's moving. My best bet is to let him come all the way in. Let him think I'm in my bedroom. Follow him. And then close in. There won't be anywhere for him to run.

The deadbolt clicks.

I snap to attention.

The knob turns, and the door pushes open slowly. It doesn't even make a sound. I think of all the nights I've slept here, oblivious, while he probably came in and watched me. Touched my cat. Fury flashes through me. I lift my chin.

Eli steps inside. In the dark, it's hard to make out his face, but he isn't even wearing a ski mask or anything like that. Cocky motherfucker. He glances around, his eyes unadjusted to the dark. His head swivels in the direction of the light peeking out from under my bedroom door. I can't see it, but I know he's smiling, that blank clicking spinning in his eyes.

My blood freezes at the thought of it.

He heads toward my door, his footfalls silent. With each pace, my nerves tighten. If I move too early, he'll see me and it'll all be over. But if I'm not fast enough, it's over anyway.

Eli stops just outside my bedroom. Silhouetted against the light, he looks like a breathing horror movie poster. He stands there for what feels like ages. I don't know how much he can see inside, but I have a feeling he already knows I'm not in there.

I don't think I'm going to get another chance.

I sidestep along the wall, then loop around in what I hope is his blind spot. The whole time, I have the gun drawn on him. He might be bigger and faster, but I'll make sure I at least put a few holes in him before he kills me.

Inching behind him, I take aim at the back of his head. When I'm only a few feet away, he swivels around.

I jump back, stifling the scream in my throat. It comes out as a wheezing gasp. "Don't move," I say, the gun still trained on him.

I expect him to lunge at me, but he just stands there. Several beats pass. Neither of us move. Eli doesn't speak.

"What do you want?" I ask, even though I don't really expect an answer. It's obvious what he wants.

The living room light flicks on, flooding my vision. I shut my eyes against the burn, taking several steps back. Eli's laugh skewers me. Jerking my eyes open, I point the gun right at his face.

His hand lowers from the light switch next to my bedroom door. Turning his arms, he exposes his forearms to me, sleeves already rolled up.

Nausea creeps up my throat as my eyes trace the letters of my name that are carved into his flesh. The wounds are still raw, as if he did it only hours ago.

"I love you, Olivia," he breathes. "I want to take your picture."

My stomach curdles. "Sorry, but I'm not into modeling." I'm impressed by how steady my voice is.

He reaches into his back pocket and pulls out a stack of

photos. With one flick of his wrist, he drops them to the floor. They scatter, and I can clearly see the subject.

Dio, sitting on his haunches, big eyes looking into the camera.

Dio, bloody and mangled on my bed.

Me, unlocking my front door, my face turned to the side.

Esther's slit tires, the Valentine's message carved into her trunk.

Me, asleep in my bed, curls framing my face.

The air comes out of my lungs in a whoosh.

"I wanted to touch you," Eli says, "brush your hair back. But I was afraid you'd wake up. You look so peaceful when you sleep." The smile that spreads across his face is waxy and off balance, as if someone pinned it into place. "But I really want to shoot you while you're awake."

He reaches into his back pocket again, pulling out a small black rectangular object. I've seen enough movies to know what it is. Before I can squeeze off a round, he pulls the trigger.

Electricity grips me, convulsing through me. Despite how tightly I hold onto it, the gun drops to the floor. I crumple right after it. Shockwaves jerk every nerve and muscle in my body. Blood oozes from my nose. The pain is seemingly never-ending.

Eli looms over me. "Hmn. I may have turned that up too high." Pocketing the taser, he grabs my wrists and drags me into the living room. "We'll set up a studio right here." His voice is delirious with joy. "Don't move, sweetheart. I'll be right back."

I hear the front door open and close. Gasping, I will my muscles to move. It's life or death here. But they don't so much as twitch. If I could cry, I would—but there's no time anyway. I try to wiggle a toe, anything. Nothing happens.

I wish I'd paid more attention during the self-defense class I took as a freshman.

I focus on breathing, bringing oxygen into my paralyzed body. Breathing out the toxins from the electricity. Seconds race by. Eli can't have much equipment. I've got to hurry.

The feeling in my muscles starts to creep back in. Agonizing pain grips me. Gritting my teeth, I raise myself up onto my elbows. I army crawl through the living room, sweat pouring down my face and back. It doesn't matter. Fuck the pain. If I don't reach that gun, I'm dead.

I near the gun. It's only a few feet away.

The front door swings open.

Launching myself forward, I grab the weapon. Eli springs across the living room, a heavy boot kicking at my arm. I squeeze off a round, but it goes wild. The silencer mutes it, but the impact of the bullet into one of Esther's vases is ear shattering. Glass flies everywhere, shards glittering on the floor. I swing my arms back, using my knees to retreat a few feet. I need room, but Eli reaches for me.

I pull the trigger, embedding a bullet in his hand.

He screams in pain, his other hand gripping his wrist as if the limb is going to fall off and he'd better hold on. As if sensing that I'm aiming again, this time to kill, he dives toward me.

I roll onto my side, skittering out of the way just in time. He crashes into the coffee table. Several candles in heavy jars go flying. One thuds into his shoulder. Groaning, he grabs it and chucks it at me. It slams into my temple.

The room goes gray, spins.

Gritting my teeth, I force myself to stay here. Blood streams down my forehead, into my eye, cascading down my cheek. I blink away the burning pain.

Eli throws himself at me, his good hand clamping around my ankle. He starts to drag me forward, face red with exertion. "I'm going to break your hands and then carve out your insides," he laughs, "and then I'm going to shoot you. I'm going to shoot you," he grunts over and over.

Bringing up the gun, I take aim at his face. "Fuck that," I force out. I squeeze the trigger. The bullet slams into the space between his eyes, leaving a quiet hole. He jerks back, eyes widening in surprise. For a moment, his grip on my ankle tightens. Then he careens back. Open eyes gape up at the ceiling. He doesn't move.

Blood seeps into the white carpet.

All at once, my entire body starts shaking. I can't move or think. All I can see is the puddle of inky red and that perfect entry wound. Then my vision goes gray.

I slap myself, hard. I actually see stars, my cheek stinging from the impact. But it does the trick. Dropping the gun, I cling to the wall, using it to draw myself to my feet. I stagger toward the front door.

Eli left it partially open. I peer out into the night. My apartment complex and neighborhood sit in silence. It's as if none of this has actually happened. I shut the door and face my living room.

My eyes go instantly to the body on my floor, as if magnetized. It starts to sink in. I've just killed a man. There's a corpse in my apartment.

A sob builds in my throat, but I cut it off. This is no time to cry. I've got work to do. I have to get rid of Eli. The problem is, I've never done this before. I have no clue what I'm doing. Plus, my arms and legs might as well be spaghetti, thanks to the taser. I need help.

And there's only one person I can trust.

17

CLIFF

The shrill ring of my phone jerks me out of a dead sleep. I sit up in bed, sweating. The club rooms are hot, as if the hormones from downstairs rise, permeating the ceiling that separates the two floors. Swinging my legs over the edge, I get up and crack a window. Cold air rushes in. Heavy lidded, I tip my head back and enjoy the wave.

My phone rings again. Silently cursing Lucy for choosing such a bone shattering ringtone, I scoop it from the nightstand.

The name on the display makes all of the blood drain straight out of my head. Before I even answer, I already know. Something is wrong.

"Are you okay?" I ask.

"Cliff," she gasps. "Please."

There's no need for her to say any more.

I pull on clothes as I make my way through the small room, shrugging into my cut almost as an afterthought. I pound down the stairs and fly out the door. It's as if my body has taken control, leaving my brain in my bed. By the time my head catches up, I'm flying down 63.

I ignore the speed limit and get to Olivia's in under ten

minutes. It's probably more like five. Practically knocking the motorcycle over, I dismount and break into a run.

The apartment door is unlocked. I push my way in and look around wildly for her. My brain processes the scene in small increments.

Blood on the carpet in the entryway.

Shattered knick knacks strewn across the floor.

Olivia huddled next to her bedroom door, a gash oozing from her temple.

The Glock in her lap.

A man splayed in the center of the living room, a hole between his eyes.

I rock back on my heels, the wind knocked out of my lungs. Memories assault me: another house, another body on the floor, another girl curled into a corner. Shaking them away, I go to her. My hands cup her face, turning her head gently so I can see the wound. "What happened?" The flesh at her temple is split wide open, blood pulsing from within. She'll need stitches, and it'll probably scar, but it doesn't look life threatening.

The chalky pallor of her face is what worries me. Her eyes slide from mine toward the body in the middle of the floor.

Following her gaze, I realize I recognize him. "That's the guy from the gas station," I say, turning back to her. "Olivia. Tell me what happened."

"What are we going to do with him?" Her voice is eerily calm. Those eyes burn into mine, pupils constricted to tiny pinpricks.

For the first time, I notice the tiny punctures marring her neck, arms, and legs. I take her wrists, holding them up. Her limbs are limp in my grasp. "What the fuck happened, Olivia?"

She gazes down. "Oh, *those*. I had to yank the barbs out." She laughs. "I don't know how the fuck I crawled around with those things in."

"Okay." I pull her into my lap, wrapping my arms around her.

"You're in shock. It's okay." Stroking her hair, I press safety into her.

My mind whirls. Distantly, I think that I may be in shock, too. Again I look at the body. Another gunshot wound pierces the hand curled next to his face. My Olivia did this. Sending her away only dragged her in deeper.

It's all my fault.

Jaw flexing, I consider my options. There's no question. I have to take care of this. Too much time has already passed. I lift the gun from the floor, nodding when I see the filed-off serial number. If we call the police, they'll quickly conclude that this was premeditated, not self-defense. My girl will go away.

Coiled nerves clamor for a cigarette. Lifting Olivia into my arms, I stand and carry her into the bedroom so that we can smoke without having to look at the body. I sit her down on the bed. Then I light two and pass her one.

"Breaking all kinds of rules today," she says with a sigh.

I lean against the vanity, thinking. I can send her away, to the store or something. Call the police and tell them that I was waiting for her to get back when this motherfucker broke in. He came at me, and I had no choice. But the crime scene is set up all wrong, and their forensics team will discover the truth.

Olivia will still go to prison.

I can re-stage it, take the fall. I don't want to go back in, but she has so much more to lose. It was probably only a matter of time anyway. Still, it would separate us. There would be no one to keep her safe. The club might be looking out for her, but they don't care for her like I do. And I'm of no use to her buried under all of that concrete.

There's really only one option here.

I think of Bree, the bruises around her neck and her cavalier attitude. "No one. Not anymore," she said. If the River Reapers can make a long line of abusive men disappear, they can manage one more.

But I'm not sure. The men who beat on Bree were nobodies. Probably alcoholics, at least unemployed. The kind of people who are easy to erase, people so toxic, no one will miss them. Not this guy. Eli was a college student, a guy who worked at a gas station. There are plenty of people who will notice he's gone.

"Fuck," I mutter. I rub my eyes with the heels of my hands.

Olivia tips her head back, those intense eyes meeting mine. "You have to call Donny."

She's right. As the club Enforcer, he'll know what to do. I may only be a Prospect, but I'm already a part of the club. It's only a matter of time. And since the club considers Olivia family too, via her connection to me and who her father is, this is official club business.

The price we'll pay will be heavy, though.

I call Donny, hoping his ringtone is just as annoying as mine. Lifting the cigarette to my lips, I suck in a drag, but it's gone out. I relight it, counting the trills on the other end of the line.

He answers on the third ring. "What is it?" he rasps, voice thick with sleep.

"We have a . . . situation over at Olivia's," I say.

Several seconds slip by. "Fuck." He exhales sharply. "All right, Red Dog. You're gonna stay put and wait for me. Comprende?"

"Yeah."

"Fuck," he says again. "How bad is it?"

I stick my head out of the bedroom, re-sweeping the scene. "Some blood. Mostly a clean shot. She did good."

He sputters. "*She*? Shit, man." He grunts. "I'll be right there. Stay put." Then he hangs up.

My eyes meet Olivia's. "Donny's on his way."

She nods once. "My head really hurts." Raising her hand to the gash on her face, she presses the pads of her fingers to the split flesh. A wince scrunches her face. "Right." Her hand flops back into her lap.

"Head wounds always bleed so much more than limbs do," I

say, eyeing it. The bleeding has slowed, which is a good sign. But every time she moves her face, a fresh wave gushes out. "You've got to try to stay still." I start hunting for something to compress it.

I find towels, rubbing alcohol, and a mostly useless first aid kit in the bathroom. There aren't even any butterfly bandages. All she and her roommate have are finger-sized Disney princess Band-Aids and a few large bandages. Still, I take it all with me back into her room.

"How do you feel?" I ask while I clean her up.

"Fine." Her eyebrows furrow. "I think."

"You've got to stop moving your face." I press a wadded up towel to the gash on her temple, using all of my weight. "Are you dizzy at all?"

"No." She closes her eyes, her face becoming a smooth mask. "I feel . . . a rush."

"Yeah." I bow my head, heart seizing in my chest. I know exactly what she's talking about. Maybe there was no stopping this, but I feel responsible. Like I should have just stuck around.

Her eyes open, latching mine. "Do you still want me to stay away?" Her voice is low, a caress across my soul.

I shake my head. "I do want you to stay still, though." Gently, I hold her chin with my free hand.

She rolls her eyes, but a tiny smile lifts the corners of her mouth. "You should've been a doctor."

"Right." I peel away the towel. The bleeding has stopped, but I'm pretty sure it's just going to split open again the second she lifts an eyebrow. Which will be any minute now, knowing my expressive girl. I dab rubbing alcohol on it. Even though it has to sting, she takes it all in stride, even as I smear Vaseline on it.

"That was all we had, huh?" She sighs softly. "I really need to invest in some Neosporin."

I stick one of the large bandages on it, trying to contour it to her hairline. "We've gotta find someone who can give you stitches."

"I'm not going to the hospital." Her chin juts out at me.

"I wasn't suggesting that." My gaze softens. Even gushing blood, she's the most headstrong person I've ever met.

A knock sounds at the front door. "Honey, I'm home," Donny calls.

"In here." I take Olivia's hand and give it a squeeze. "Don't worry. It's gonna be okay." Pressing a kiss to her lips, I stand and meet Donny in the living room.

But it isn't just Donny.

Beer Can drops a huge duffel bag at my feet. He nods in greeting.

"Let's get to work, boys," Donny says.

Stepping over the body, he leers down at it. "Not a lot of blood. Good. That'll be easy to clean up." He lifts the hand that Olivia shot. "And look, part of my job is already done for me." Looking over his shoulder, he grins at me. "Grab me that tarp from that duffel bag."

Hunkering down, I unzip the bag. Before I look away from Donny, though, I realize he's wearing a patch I've never seen before. "What's a Sludge Specter?"

He just smiles and goes back to examining the body.

I carry the tarp over. "So what are you going to do?"

"Me?" Donny's eyebrows lift. "This is a team effort. It takes a lot of muscle to dismantle a man. It is a little easier if you saw at the joints, though." He winks.

Grimacing, I take several bone saws out of the duffel bag. I hold one out to Beer Can.

He shakes his head, holding up his hands. "I'm just the cleaning lady."

"What can I do?" Olivia asks from the bedroom door.

Both of the men gape at her.

"Jesus Christ," Beer Can says in a low voice.

The bandage on her temple is already soaked through.

I try to see her through their eyes. With half her face covered in sticky blood, her T-shirt damp and wrinkled with sweat and more blood, and body pocked with barb holes, she's a pretty ghastly sight. But long, bare legs extend from underneath that T-shirt, and hard nipples press against the cotton. Those luminous eyes tunnel through me, and all I want to do is kiss those soft, full lips and solidify my claim to her.

But we have work to do.

"I'll call Ravage," Beer Can says, pressing a phone to his ear.

"Liv, you probably shouldn't see this." I step in front of her, blocking her view.

She snorts. "Because it'll be traumatic? Cliff, I *did* this. I shot holes through a person." Her voice drops to a whisper. "And you know what? I liked it, just like you said. It felt good. *Right.*"

"Yeah." Taking her by the shoulders, I lead her to the couch. I press down, coaxing her into a sitting position. "You're bleeding, Olivia. Ravage will come and stitch you up."

"Come on, Red Dog," Donny calls. "I need a hand getting this tarp under this fucker."

"Stay put," I order her. Joining Donny, I pull on the gloves he passes me. He shows me how to roll the body from side to side while he inches the tarp underneath. Then he nods toward the duffel bag. I grab the two bone saws and hand him one.

"Nah," he says, taking the other from me. "This one has a better handle. Fits better to my hand," he explains. I wonder how many times he's done this, but I don't ask. I probably don't want to know.

Donny demonstrates how to separate an elbow, angling the saw into the soft inside of the joint. "This is where the tendon connects." He thrusts it forward, using his weight to drive the serrated blade into the flesh. "Skin and muscle cuts like butter," he says, watching as blood puddles below the arm. "But you need a little more force to get through the joint." He drives in, the muscles in his arm bunching. The blade makes a sickening wet popping sound as it slides through the joint.

I stare, feeling as if I'm watching all of this from outside myself. It's partially fascinating and also kind of disgusting. And, if i'm being honest, it's unsettling how someone as warm and friendly as Donny can do this so easily. Like it's second nature.

He beckons to a leg. "Join the party, Red Dog."

We get to work.

I feel myself disconnecting as I grip the calf and twist until the back of the knee comes around. The hip pops out of socket almost too easily. Pressing the bone saw into the back of the knee, I tell myself this isn't real. It's just something I have to do and can forget about when it's all over. I separate what I'm doing and my real life into halves as cleanly as I'm dismembering joints. Time becomes irrelevant as Donny and I work side by side in silence.

I don't even hear Ravage come in.

An hour and forty-five minutes later, we have a pile of bloody limbs, skin hanging from all ends in tattered shreds.

"All right," Donny says. "That's the easy part. Now we've gotta break these down. Convenient pieces, brother. Fun Size." Laughter dances in his eyes, his grin wide.

"You're enjoying this too much," I grunt.

Before I dive back in, I glance at Olivia. She's sitting cross-legged on the couch next to Ravage, who hands her a cup of tea. Neat stitches line her temple, and her face is clean. She looks human again.

I look down at my own hands. The gloves only come up to my wrists, so my arms and everything I'm wearing is soaked in blood. Now I *look* like a monster.

Donny pulls a giant pair of industrial cutters out of his magic bag. He scissors the blades, metal clicking against metal. Following his lead, I hold body parts while he cuts them down. Blood splashes my face. After a little while, I stop caring. The whole time, I feel Olivia's eyes on me.

What will become of us when this is over?

I don't think any less of her, but I'm not so sure she feels the same about me. We're past the point of walking away, though. Whatever happens next, this night has bound us together.

All of us.

"I'm going back to bed," Ravage says, lifting a hand in parting. "Call me if you run into any problems." He strides out the door as if we're just mopping floors in here.

Donny was right. Sawing through joints is much easier than it is to go through straight bone. There's beauty in that stubborn strength, though. I feel a new appreciation for my own body as I get down on one knee and drag the bone saw back and forth.

Two more hours pass with Beer Can brewing us coffee and sitting with Olivia. Despite the late hour, I'm not at all tired. From the looks of the others, neither are they.

"So where's Esther?" I ask Donny, swiping sweat from my forehead with a bloody arm. It doesn't even matter at this point.

"Essie?" His face drifts off, dreams in his eyes. "She's at the hotel. I told her I'd be back sometime tomorrow."

"Sorry I ruined your weekend," Olivia says from the couch.

"Nah." Donny gives her a gentle smile. "I'd do anything for you, girl. You know that."

Beer Can grunts in agreement.

Finally Donny declares the chunks an appropriate size. Even the smell doesn't bother me anymore. I hold a giant, heavy duty Ziploc bag open while he tosses them in.

From the duffel bag, Beer Can pulls out an industrial blender.

"Fuck me," I mutter.

He plugs it into the wall, putting a clean tarp underneath it. Then he motions for me to get started, as if gesturing for a lady to go first through a door.

More pieces of me fragment as I feed chunks of Eli to the machine. Donny holds another Ziploc open for me to pour the puree into. When I'm done, I sit back on my knees, breathing heavily.

"You got this?" Donny asks Beer Can.

"Never underestimate a Virgo," Beer Can says, shooing us away.

I reach for the duffel bag.

"Leave it." Donny shakes his head. "Beer Can'll bring it back to me when they're done." He beckons for me to follow him.

Outside, we climb into his truck. The seats and floors have been covered with tarps, the steering wheel and shift wrapped in kitchen plastic wrap.

I whistle. "You've really thought this through."

"It's my job," he says, backing out of his spot.

We drive deep into the woods of Naugatuck, to a piece of property tucked away from civilization. Carrying the bag, I follow Donny through an unmarked and overgrown trail into a clearing. A bonfire is already going in a large pit.

"Throw it in." He yanks off his bloodied clothing and tosses it onto the flames. "You too. Everything but the cut." Then he goes to the truck and collects the tarps.

This night can't get any more bizarre.

As the flames lick the dismembered flesh, a pungent stench fills the air. I stand naked next to an equally bare Donny, wearing nothing but our leather vests, huddling near the flames for warmth. The ground is cold on my feet, but after a while they go numb. I wish I'd thought to bring cigarettes, but I guess I'll have plenty of time to chainsmoke the night away later.

It's another hour, maybe two, before the fire burns out. Donny scoops the ashes into another big Ziploc using a shovel, then tucks the bag among the roots of a tree.

The sky begins to lighten.

"So what now?" I cross my arms, feeling more cold than I want to admit. I need sex, whiskey, a cigarette, and a long dead sleep.

Headlights dance through the trees. My spine stiffens. I look at Donny. He turns toward the incoming truck, shoulders relaxed.

The truck parks next to Donny's and a hollow-eyed man jumps out. Within minutes, he erects a showering tent and connects a tank of water to it. He hands me a fresh bar of soap. "In you go, son."

The water is surprisingly hot. Almost scalding, actually. I scrub blood from my skin and underneath my nails, washing my hair three times before I'm certain that all of the chunks of flesh and bone are gone. When I step out, the unnamed man hands me a bundle of clothing and work boots. They're even the right size.

Donny showers next.

I watch as our friend collects the bag of ashes and throws them into the back of the pickup. "What are you gonna do with that?" I ask him.

He snuffles and hawks a wad of spit. Instead of blowing it out, though, he swallows. "Gonna mix it into my manure," he says.

Joining us, Donny slings an arm around me. "He's our local manure man."

"Thank you for supporting a small business," the man says. He pours the remainder of the water in the tank, rinsing the shower. Then he takes a bucket from his truck and dumps some kind of cleaner all over the tent. It's too dark to make out what it is. "I'll air this out at home."

Donny claps him on the back. "Thanks, man." He motions for me to get in the truck.

We drive back to Olivia's in silence. My eye twitches every few seconds, an old signal that I've gone too long without sleep. I think of all the dirty secrets that tie Olivia and me together, and wonder if that's enough of a bond for a real new beginning.

18

Dawn rises, and with it Cliff returns. He's wearing different clothes, and his face is haggard. I snuggle into his arms.

"Thank you," I whisper.

He presses a kiss to the top of my head. "It looks good in here," he says over me.

I nod. Beer Can did most of the work, but I helped a little. We used meat tenderizer and some enzyme soap to get the stains out of the carpet, then he peeled it back and scrubbed the concrete underneath. Luckily it wasn't stapled—whoever did the carpeting just tucked it in a little around the kick molding. "Apparently my landlord's even more of a cheapskate than I thought," I say to Cliff.

But it worked in our favor. Beer Can collected everything—including my beloved MSI T-shirt—and put it all in a heavy duty garbage bag, promising that he'd take care of it. I didn't ask how, and I don't want to know.

Cliff ducks his head, meeting my eyes. "Are you okay?" His voice is husky.

Nodding slowly, I pull off the fresh T-shirt I'd changed into after Beer Can made me shower. "Please touch me," I whisper.

He palms one of my breasts, the rough underside of his hand grazing my nipple. His eyes meet mine, hooded but tender.

My hands go to the button of his pants, releasing it from its hole. I unzip them and wrap my fingers around him. He throbs, hot in my grasp. "Cliff," I plead, giving him a tug. I lead him toward the bedroom, leaving the scene of the crime I've committed.

Solemn, he stands before me, watching me.

I hook an arm around his neck, pulling his face to mine. I lay myself down, drawing him on top of me. Holding himself above me, his lips glide across mine, and the already aching need in me soaks my panties. I reach for him and push him inside. My legs wrap around his waist as he thrusts home. Deeper and deeper he drives, my nails digging into the flesh of his back.

I turn and sink my teeth into the tenderness of his neck, marking him.

"Who's too dangerous, now?" I whisper into his ear as he glides in and out, pushing me to the edge.

"I won't leave you again," he rumbles. He lifts me and wraps his arms around me.

And just like that we are bound, he and I, by our past, present, and future. Neither death nor time can separate us. He is mine, and I am his.

Forever.

WE SLEEP for the rest of the day. I miss my classes, and I don't care. I cocoon myself in his arms and under blankets, getting up only to pee and check on Dio, who has the run of the place again.

We order in meals and for the most part leave our clothes off.

It's like we can't get enough of each other, bodies tangling in fevered passion. I don't even worry about cooling it anymore, or my rules, and he doesn't try to tell me that we shouldn't be together.

We just are.

Around eight o'clock, Cliff gets a call from Ravage. "He wants both of us at the club," he tells me. "For Church."

This should alarm me, but all I care about is that we're together. Since he doesn't seem too concerned, I decide not to worry about it.

We shower together, Cliff lifting me and fucking me against the warm tile. Then, dressing, he and I get ready to face the club. We mount the Screamin' Eagle and tear toward The Wet Mermaid, the wind in our ears drowning out our thoughts. I feel more connected to him than I ever have to anyone else. Maybe it's in my head.

Or maybe the couple that makes people disappear together stays together.

The only vehicles in the parking lot are motorcycles and club-owned cars and pickups. It's a bit unnerving that they closed down The Wet Mermaid for this meeting—that they couldn't wait 'til after hours. Swallowing hard, I look at Cliff. He shrugs and takes my hand, wrapping my fingers in his warmth.

Stepping inside, I note the somber mood of the place. Shadows drift across the floor and stage. Cliff leads me to the bar and, without letting go of my hand, makes us drinks. We carry them into the conference room, joining the rest of the men for Church.

They sit around the heavy wooden table, Ravage at the head. The other members nod at us as we come in. I avoid Donny's gaze. It still weirds me out that the guy who is banging my friend is the same guy who dismembered a body like it was nothing, then referred to the pieces as "Fun Size."

Cliff and I take the two empty seats near the end, and Ravage calls the meeting to order.

"We had a bit of a situation last night," he says, eyes drifting over his River Reapers. "As you may have heard."

Mark nods emphatically. He won't look at me. The lines of his mouth are hard and I can't tell whether he's angry with me. The men sitting around this table are completely different from the men I've been working with.

"Donny. Mark." Ravage says their names sharply. "Our Enforcer and our Treasurer gave this young lady one of our guns." Shaking his head, he rubs his temples. "Without my permission." The glare he gives Donny and Mark is full of venom. Then, his stare softens. "But they did the right thing, gentlemen— under the circumstances. Because Olivia here is just like her damn father." His flat look transfers to me. "Always wanting to handle everything on their own, these fucking Reynolds."

Cliff's hand squeezes mine, and I'm grateful that he's with me. I have a feeling that I'm about to be fired. Even though Mark owns the strip club on paper, it's MC property. Even though I'm the one who killed Eli, I still compromised the club.

Ravage's eyes settle on Cliff. "Son, I opened my club to you. Gave you a job, a room to sleep in." He lights a cigarette. Over the red glow of the tip, he says, "The two of you dragged this club into a shit storm."

My eyes close for a second. It didn't occur to me that they might kick Cliff out. Before he was even in. I bow my head.

"We took a vote," Ravage continues. "It was unanimous. But I want to say that this isn't how I wanted shit to go. This should have been a long process."

My eyebrows furrow, my temple throbbing in pain. "What's going on?"

The President nods to Cliff. "Give me that cut," he growls.

Cliff nods. "It's okay," he says to me. Standing, he shrugs it off. He folds it in half and carries it over to Ravage. "I understand." He touches Ravage's shoulder. "No hard feelings."

Scowling, Ravage swats his hand away. He pulls a knife from

an interior pocket of his own leather vest. Then, with a surgeon's precision, he cuts the stitches that hold the Prospect rocker to Cliff's cut. He looks balefully up at Cliff. "Do you know what this means, son?"

One of Cliff's eyebrows twitch, but he says nothing. Just nods.

Ravage slides two patches over to him. Squinting, I read the words MEMBER on one and SLUDGE SPECTER on the other. "Welcome, son." He stands and embraces Cliff. "Don't fuck this up." He claps Cliff on the back.

"Guess I'm gonna have to learn how to sew." Cliff holds up the patches and his vest. The men pound on the table, laughing and insulting his manhood. Returning to his seat next to me, Cliff again takes my hand.

My shoulders relax. I figure, since Cliff didn't get kicked out, I probably still have a job. Even then, it wouldn't be the worst thing in the world—as much as I love working at The Wet Mermaid.

"Olivia," Ravage says, my name almost an exasperation on his lips. He jerks his head. "Get up here."

Despite my confusion, I manage to keep my face still. The wound is still tender as fuck, plus it feels really weird when the stitches pull. I stand and cross the room to the head of the table, passing men who feel more like family than my own parents.

Maybe it's because, despite the years that separate us, they *are* family.

Stopping at Ravage's side, I brace myself for whatever's coming. Maybe he's going to tell me that I have to stay away from Cliff. I lift my chin. He can try.

He crosses his arms. "Your father always had big ideas for this club. Something about straddling the line between the ninety-nine and the one percent. And he wanted to change certain . . . other things. He wanted you to be a part of it."

I blink. Tilting my head, my lips part.

Ravage holds up a hand. "It *is* the 21st Century, for Christ's sake. We had to take another vote, though—you know, as a formality. It was also unanimous."

Mark stands and joins us. He hands me a leather vest folded in half—small compared to the men's.

Lips parted, I unfold it. My fingers trace the Prospect rocker that will curve just under my ribs. "How?" I'm breathless with awe. This shouldn't be happening. It's never happened before in any MC, as far as I know.

"It's your heritage," Ravage replies. "Both of you. Though it's a hell of a lot sooner than I'd planned." He fixes Cliff and me with a look somewhere between annoyed and proud. Then he turns back to me. "Beer Can will hook you up with a ride and get you started."

I lift an eyebrow at him, trying to imagine myself riding a motorcycle. "Or I can just ride with Cliff."

Ravage looks like I've just kicked his elderly mother. "We all ride," he snarls, his smoke and whiskey laced voice ringing out through the room.

The other men nod in agreement, their jaws set. Their serious facial expressions are pretty comical, but it would be really disrespectful to laugh at them.

"Okay, so no room for negotiation there." I hold up the vest. "Thanks." Biting back a smile, I go back to my seat. Cliff smirks and slings an arm around my shoulders.

"This is monumental, kid," Ravage tells me across the table. "Don't fuck it up." He gives me a single, very stern nod. I guess this is his way of asking me to please not kill anymore college students.

I lift my shoulders and, pressing my lips together, smile apologetically. "I'll do my best."

The meeting ends shortly after. I'm not allowed to attend regular Church, but this evening was an exception. Ravage fills us in on an upcoming ride for charity in the spring, with a remark about how I'll have plenty of time to learn how to ride before then.

Following Cliff out of the conference room, I head straight to the bar for another drink.

"Already?" he jokes, his hand resting on the small of my back.

"I'm under a lot of pressure now, okay?" I toss him a smile to let him know that I'm really not worried. If Beer Can could teach Cliff how to ride, he can totally teach me. Probably. "I wouldn't put it past Ravage to lend me the biggest bike there is." I pout, sipping my vodka collins.

"That would be pretty hot, though." Cliff grins slyly. "Tiny girl on a big bike?" He grabs my hips and presses my ass against him, his erection hard through his jeans. "I'm turned on just from the thought," he growls into my ear.

I put my unfinished drink down on the bar and toss a few bills as an extra tip to the bartender. "Let's get you home, then, so I can ride *you*."

On the way back to my place, I hug Cliff tight and press my thighs into the purring machine beneath me. It's an awful lot of power to bestow on someone. I close my eyes, feeling the engine thrum through my body. This life wasn't something that I ever thought I wanted, but now that it's mine, I don't ever want to give it back.

I think of my father, sifting through the murky, blurred memories that I have of him. Finally I have an explanation for why he was in and out of my life. It *must* have been the club. Nothing else would have kept him away from me and Mom.

Thinking of her brings a pang to my chest. Ever since the day I was taken away, I've tried hard not to dwell on her at all. It was better for everyone if I just pretended like Lucy and her parents were my real family—even when I was still just their foster kid. But the truth hits me hard out here on the road.

Family is about more than just how you look. A family means a whole lifestyle, a real place to belong. From my mannerisms to the things I gravitate to, it's all ingrained in me. Nothing can change that, not even thirteen years apart.

Cliff slows as we enter the parking lot. When the motorcycle stops, I hug him tight. Then I hop down.

"Come on in and show me just how bad you are, *Red Dog*," I tease, backing toward the front door. I withdraw my key and turn it in the lock, grateful that I don't have to worry about finding surprises when I come home anymore.

Cliff clears his throat as he comes in behind me. "Actually, I need to talk to you about something."

"Sure," I say, tossing my coat onto the floor. I lift my sweater off over my head. "I can multitask." A wolfish grin splits my face. I want to devour him. Ever since he's walked into my life, I haven't been able to get enough. It's not just the sex, even though I've never had such gravity-defying orgasms before.

He catches my arm, drawing me into his embrace. "In a minute." Those lips press a kiss to the tip of my nose. Wrapping an arm around my waist, he leads me to the couch. Then he pulls me into his lap.

I straddle him, the heat from my core sparking against his hot erection pressing against me. I roll my hips, greedy.

A smile tugs at his lips. He stills my waist, though. "This is serious, babe." After a beat, he continues. "I saw your mom."

The breath catches in my throat. I sit back, my hands resting on his shoulders. "Where?" is all I can think to say.

"Prospect duty." His lips twitch to the side. "You're in for it, Liv. They had me doing all kinds of errands. The other day, I had to bring this woman to catch a train out of New Haven."

"Bree." Her name is a prayer on my lips. Tears sting my eyes. "How did she look? What did she say?" A thousand more questions tumble through my head. I don't know where she's been. I wish I knew why she didn't fight for me. I really want to know why she hasn't tried to look me up since I turned eighteen. All of these questions burst through the surface of the placid exterior

I've been trying to maintain. Up until now, I had no idea that it all bothered me so much.

The emotions ripping through me are overwhelming.

Using the pad of his thumb, Cliff brushes away my tears. "It's okay," he says quietly. "And *she's* okay. I mean, she had some bruises. The club obviously sent her out of state—"

I hold up a hand. "Bruises? Again?" My head throbs, and it's not just the healing slash at my temple.

He nods. "Don't worry. Whoever he was, he won't be a problem anymore."

I press my lips together. Donny's been a busy man. "Where was she going?" I hate how small my voice sounds. I don't want to be a little girl who needs her mother. But it doesn't matter how hard I fight it. Knowing that Bree is alive awakens something in me, a longing buried over a decade ago but easily unearthed.

Family is forever.

"I don't know," Cliff admits. "I'm sorry, babe. I had no idea who she was up until the second she walked away."

A bitter snort erupts from my nostrils. "Sounds about right." Sighing, I snuggle into his arms. "But she looked okay, otherwise?"

"Yes." He kisses the top of my head. Strong arms wrap around me, hugging me close. Again it overwhelms me how right this is, how perfectly we fit together. I'm not ready to drop the L word or to throw a ring on it and pop out babies, but *this* is enough. It's everything I've ever wanted.

Except for one thing.

"I want to find her." Sitting up, I zero in on his eyes so that he knows I'm serious. I have no idea where to start. She doesn't have a Facebook. I've searched for her before. Ravage has to know something, though. "They dropped all kinds of information on me about Mercy, but they couldn't bother to tell me about Bree." My lip curls. "It's awfully convenient."

A wry smile drags Cliffs lips to the side, his eyebrows raised as he nods in agreement. "Try not to blame them, though." He pauses, considering. "Or us. Is that how this works? Cogs in a single unit?"

"More like a pack of wolves." I run my fingers through his long black hair. "I don't know, Cliff. I feel like there's a whole hell of a lot more that they haven't told me."

"You're just a Prospect," he says. "Give it time. I'll talk to Ravage. Or Beer Can. He's much more forthcoming. Especially after a few beers. Is that why they call him Beer Can?"

Cheeks reddening, I snort laugh. It quickly turns into a series of giggles. My eyes close and my lips press together, belly shaking. When I finally get myself under control, I open my eyes. Cliff lifts a bushy eyebrow at me. "It's not because of what he drinks," I manage with a straight face. "It's because his, um . . ."

"Say no more. Please." Cliff's face turns to stone and he glances away. "Next subject."

Cupping his chin, the short beard tickling the palm of my hand, I turn his face back to me. "You're my in. They trust you now. Anything you find out, I have to know." I'm practically begging, but I'm desperate. If Bree is in trouble, I need to be informed so I can help her. Despite how she's let me down, she shouldn't be on her own. And the club doesn't count.

Muscular arms wrap around me. "Of course, Olivia," he says in a husky voice. "I would do anything for you."

"I know," I reply, because I do.

The End

GET MORE OLIVIA & CLIFF

The next book in the River Reapers series, *A Risky Prospect*, is under way!

PRE-ORDER NOW
Pre-order your copy now at **books2read.com/ariskyprospect**

Here are other things you can do while you wait.

POST A REVIEW

Tell everyone how much you loved *A Disturbing Prospect* in a review! Visit **books2read.com/adisturbingprospect** to select a review website.

JOIN THE OFFICIAL FAN CLUB

Get notified when *A Risky Prospect* is live, plus get exclusive bonus content and other goodies! Visit **bit.ly/RiverReapersMCFanClub** to sign up.

Join My Reader Group

Hang out with me and other readers in my group while I finish writing *A Risky Prospect*. Visit **facebook.com/groups/baronesbelles** to join.

BODY COUNT

2

ACKNOWLEDGMENTS

A Disturbing Prospect sat on my laptop for over a year before I hit publish.

I probably wouldn't have published this book if it wasn't for J.C. Hannigan, who talked me off the ledge, oh . . . 100 times? Publishing this book is one of the scarier things I've done, but I'm speaking my truth and nothing is stopping me. Thanks, J, for reminding me of that.

When my work wife wasn't patiently talking me through my fears, it was my IRL husband, Mike Campbell. "Is this too far?" I'd ask. "Wait, why am I asking *you*?" Thank you for reinforcing my skin and helping me stay true to this book, and also for rolling with my intense late-night writing sessions.

Eternal thanks to everyone who helped me whip this book into shape, especially my critique partner and beta readers: Molli Moran, J.C. Hannigan, DeAnna Knippling, Michelle Heron, and Katy Young.

Thank you to Erica, who put me back together after I fell apart. If PTSD is a hellish journey, then you're the guide with the bright lantern and warm Thermos (and essential oils).

Thank you to CJPB Designs for the first edition cover, and Nastaha Snow for the second edition.

Finally, thank you "Lucy" for existing. I'm so glad you keep fighting to be here.

ABOUT THE AUTHOR

Elizabeth Barone is an American novelist who writes contemporary romance and suspense starring sassy belles who chose a different path in life. Her debut novel *Sade on the Wall* was a quarterfinalist in the 2012 Amazon Breakthrough Novel Award contest. She is the author of the **South of Forever** series and several other books.

When not writing, Elizabeth is very busy getting her latest fix of Yankee Candle, spicy Doritos chips, or whatever TV show she's currently binging.

Elizabeth lives in northwestern Connecticut with her husband, a feisty little cat, and too many books.

Connect with Elizabeth
https://elizabethbaronebooks.com
elizabethbaronebooks@gmail.com

facebook.com/elizabethbaronebooks

instagram.com/elizabethbarone

twitter.com/elizabethbarone

amazon.com/author/elizabethbarone

goodreads.com/elizabethbarone

bookbub.com/authors/elizabeth-barone